MESSAGES
FROM A SYRIAN JEW TRAPPED IN EGYPT

NADENE GOLDFOOT

authorHOUSE®

AuthorHouse™
1663 Liberty Drive
Bloomington, IN 47403
www.authorhouse.com
Phone: 1-800-839-8640

Published by AuthorHouse 03/21/2014

ISBN: 978-1-4918-6665-8 (sc)
ISBN: 978-1-4918-6664-1 (e)

Library of Congress Control Number: 2014903249

This book is dedicated to my wonderful facebook friend, Amram Halabi, who found himself in such a pickle of being a Syrian refugee in Egypt and knowing that he was Jewish. This book is a compilation of all the messages and skype conversations that we had over a year's time about his life. May this bright and energetic engineer find peace in this crazy barbaric world of war in the Middle East.

Contents

Prologue

May 2012

Whooooooooosh! An incoming missile hit the ground about two blocks away and caused the earth to tremble in its pain. Vick hurried as he opened his safe to get his passport and money. He had to make it fast. Packing his bags with his clothes, he looked fondly at his guitar in the corner of his bedroom, his new American style bedroom in his new home he enjoyed so much.

As he glanced at his bathroom, he thought of all the imported things he had brought in to make it just like the pictures of homes in California and had cost him so much money. Money! But what is money if you can't live like an American! He'd better take all that he had in the safe with him. Protests had been going on ever since April all over Syria. People called this the "Arab Spring."

"Resign, Resign, Bashar al-Assad," chanted the rioters. Some had thrown Molotov cocktails. "Look out, here comes the soldiers," cried another. The soldiers commenced firing on the hapless people because they were told to quell the uprising. Months had gone by with the military firing on the people in crowds. It turned into an armed rebellion. All over the country scenes like this were taking place.

"Damn!" Thirty-one year old Vick had looked in his closet one last time saying "Au Revior" to his classy Armani suit. He wouldn't need it in Egypt, that's for sure. It's always hot there, unlike his beautiful Damascus which would get cold in the winter, even had snow sometimes. The damned security forces shot people dead in Deraa and that started the last few days of violence that was spreading all over Syria. Here in Damascus there were too many protests. They all wanted the prisoners that were being held for their political beliefs to be released. They hadn't harmed anyone! He had been a prisoner once, himself. He didn't want that experience repeated, that's for sure, though he was also sure he would survive it again. He knew how to talk to those police," he thought.

"Adieu, my home! Arivederci! Salaam! I shall return to take care of you!" Vick thought hopefully, though he wasn't sure of anything for the first time in his life. March 2012, and he had to leave the job he loved with Khayyat Contracting and Trading after two years of enjoyment and good money. Damn! Last year he saw army tanks enter near this house! They were attempting to crush the anti-regime protests. So what happened? The USA and the European Union just tightened their sanctions. That made it hard at work to get supplies he needed for the building projects. Thank G-d President Assad offered the political prisoners amnesty last year.

Then he had read that the government found that 120 members of the security forces had been killed by armed gangs in Jisr al-Shughour. Troops took over the town and more than 10,000 Syrians fled to Turkey. G-d, they don't speak Arabic there. They speak Turkish! Assad promised to start a national dialogue of reform after that. It didn't help matters at all. Here he is in 2012, running to Egypt.

Hosni Mubarak had been overthrown in February after a revolt for only eighteen days. Flashes of what he saw on the TV news, of chanting of "God is Great! God is Great," came to mind. Where he was going wasn't much safer than Syria was at the moment.

"Oh well, maybe he could get in some diving in Taba," he thought. "Now, where is my carton of cigarettes?"

ONE

Past 1986

"Uncle Ahmad, why did the Jews dry up the sky last night? You said it was their fault that it did not rain. Why did they do it?"

"Shut up, Vick. They do everything we don't like. They're the cause of all our problems. They do it on purpose to make us upset! Get out of here, Jew bait!"

"Waaa!' sobbed little Amram, the one they called Vick. Vick was a popular name in Damascus. Amram had been a picky eater since he was brought into this house at the age of ten months and tossed into his step-mother's arms who almost dropped him with the shock of such a gift. He wasn't yet aware that Nola was not his real mother.

His uncles keep yelling at him that his mother is a Jew Kike.

"Where is this other mother?" The six year old kept thinking. "Why doesn't she come and take him away from these mean uncles who push him and call him names. Do boys have two mothers?"

He had no father like the other boys in first grade. He knew that his father had died when he was three years old. He had one little picture of him. Vick had just had his 6th

birthday on March 8, 1986, and no mother brought him presents except Nola, his stepmother, whom he called Nola, not mother. She never really was "mother" in his mind. She couldn't be, after what his uncles kept reminding him about being a Jew. Nola was a Muslim because she said so.

TWO

February 1982

Vick was not quite two years old when President Assad of Syria ordered his military to demolish the city of Hama in February 1982. This brought about the slogan of "Hama Rules." It came from Thomas Friedman's book, "From Beirut to Jerusalem" where he tells how the Alawites took power in 1970 and have kept the power longer than any others in Syria. Ever since he took over, with Alawites only making up 6% of the population, the Syrian Muslim Brotherhood had been active in fighting him. Abbas fought back, playing this game by his own rules that Friedman called, the Hama Rules. It so happened that Hama was the capital of the Muslim Brotherhood.

70% of Syria's population were Sunni Muslims, but there were also Shiites, Kurds and Christians living there, and Jews. However, the Jews left in a rescue operation in 1992 and 1994.

"Sami, did you hear what happened in Hama?" Asked Alaa, his brother.

"What, Alaa? What happened?"

"There was a massacre in Hama and 20,000 people were killed in it. Do you think maybe they got all the Jews there?"

"No, most of them just live in Aleppo and Damascus, here, "replied Alaa

"I suppose Assad wanted to destroy Hama because Jews might have been instigating rebellion from there," shouted George to his family from a back room.

"I don't think there's any Jews living there," said Alaa. They should have killed all the Muslim Brotherhood guys, though. It was their stronghold. They've wanted to topple the Alawite regime of Assad. So Assad had his military demolish the city. You know, Rifaat Assad was leading the charge and he turned tanks loose on Hama. It took a few weeks, but much of the city was ruined and they had killed thousands. Some parts of the city were flattened. I heard that 20,000 were killed on orders from Assad himself."

"There were some living there a long time ago, though; let me think, yes, 1829. The Jews of Hama had killed a Muslim girl and they were all expelled from that city," commented Ahmad.

"Why did they kill the little girl," asked little Yana who had joined the conversation.

"Oh, you know, they needed her blood for the Passover matzos. Usually they'd use the blood of a Christian boy, but I guess she was more available," returned Alaa.

George dropped the book he was reading on the floor with a bang, and yelled at the younger men.

"You're all crazy! Enough! That's rot. They didn't do any such thing. I know they don't eat blood, not even from a lamb or a cow. They certainly wouldn't eat the blood of a human!"

George need not be so astonished that his daughter Nola's brother-in-laws were so anti-Semitic. The Arab countries made sure that young schoolchildren were taught to hate Jews. The Syrian Minister of Education himself wrote in 1968 that "the hatred which we indoctrinate into the minds of our children from their birth is sacred."

Assad was a minority in Syria, an Alawite, a branch of Islam and was the ruler. This was similar to Lebanon's Christians who had been ruling over Muslims there. Major Hadad had been friends of Israel and helped to guard the border they both shared from PLO insurgent terrorists.

As soon as Assad took over on November 16, 1970, the Syrian branch of the Muslim Brotherhood began to plan for his overthrow. By the late 1970s, a violent guerilla war was being waged against Assad's regime as bombs went off outside Syrian government buildings or Soviet advisers or members of Assad's ruling Baath Party were shot in frequent attacks, or taken hostage. Assad responded with abductions and assassinations of its own.

Assad himself was the target of an assassination attempt on June 26, 1980, when Muslim Brotherhood members threw two hand grenades at him, and opened fire when Assad was engaged in hosting the Mali head of state. Assad survived with a foot injury; he'd kicked away one of the grenades."

"I'm convinced that you cannot be a dictator to a country when you are in the minority," pronounced George. "I liked Bachir Geemayel who was the Christian president this year in Lebanon. He became president on the 23rd of August and then was assassinated on the 14th of September. Amine Gemayel has stepped up to the plate to take over on the 23rd of September. He's Christian, too, and I hope he will live to serve out his term. These Maronite Christians have been serving as heads of state ever since 1943 when it was decided on for Lebanon. It seemed to work for them to have a minority ruler, but then the Christians are not the Alawites."

Ahmed was listening to him and answered. "Hafez al Assad has been our minority president since he took office on the 12th of March 1971. He'll never leave until he dies. By the way, his son, Bashar, just graduated from high school. I hear that he is more interested in medicine than politics, thanks be to Allah!"

Quickly and stealthily Vick's numerous uncles, his father's brothers, had stepped in and had brazenly stolen all the money Vick's father had compiled from his very lucrative business as a cattle buyer. He had traveled as far as Denmark in buying dairy cattle for Syria and was the first to ever do that. They were thieves of Vick's future and were the ones always needling Vick about having a Jew mother. Vick had never suspected what had preceded their comments as George always had spoken well of Jews. He had told him of his friendship with the shokhet, the Jewish man who was responsible for the kosher killing of cattle in the slaughter house. The idea of cutting the throat to bring instant death without pain had appealed to him, accompanied along with a special prayer. The Muslim Halal was similar but not as worried about harming the animal and causing pain though they slit the throat also. They didn't have the rule about not killing an animal in front of other animals, nor was the man like his friend as well trained. Nola's father had copied the system and had taught it to Vick, so Vick thought maybe they had been Turkish Jews at one time. They certainly felt no ill will towards Jews like many did.

Vick's father had discovered he had bone cancer in 1983 when it was too late to stop it from taking him. He hadn't left a will. He had never thought such a thing would happen to him. His greedy brothers, who weren't so successful, took advantage of the situation and got his money and many of his treasured objects in his study. Vick had been left without a pot to pee in. He had had to hit the streets and find ways to make money at an early age. He was literally an orphan.

THREE

Nearly Present

June 4, 2009 President Obama flew to Cairo, Egypt to make a speech called, "A New Beginning" at Cairo University. He said he chose Egypt because it was the country that represented the heart of the Arab world. In this speech he tried to mend the United States' relations with the Muslim world, which he wrote were "severely damaged" during the presidency of George W. Bush.

A leader of Egypt's largest opposition group, the Muslim Brotherhood, dismissed Obama's trip and said it would be "useless unless they had seen some real change in the policies of the U.S. administration toward the Arab and Islamic world." However, Obama's administration insisted that at least ten members of the Muslim Brotherhood be allowed to attend the Cairo speech even though his was an outlawed group.

"George, what do you think of the Muslim Brotherhood?" asked Vick.

"I think they're nuts," answered George honestly. "Don't you like Damascus the way it is now?"

"Of course, George. What changes do you think would happen if the Brotherhood were in charge of the government? It started in Egypt but now is pretty strong here in Syria."

"If Assad were overthrown? It would be terrible. I'd have to go to the mosque every day, not just on Friday. We'd be fighting with Israel!"

"God, that had better not ever happen," said Vick getting choked up as he had a sudden picture in his mind of Syrian tanks entering Jerusalem, the city he held in such admiration.

"I see changes happening in Egypt now that Obama made that speech about "change," said Vick sagaciously. I saw the Muslim Brotherhood members on TV sitting there taking the speech all in and can imagine they were plotting their next move. They're against Jews. Have you seen their charter?"

"I've heard. Their motto is that Jihad is their way and they are all for violent jihad. I'm not for killing to get something. They're not for talking over things; no give or take with them. They're against Israel and the United States and they think that Allah is commanding them to be violent."

"Right." answered Vick. "They want to restore the calliphate and that means going back to all the Shariah law but for the whole world this time. America would have to fall. My America! Remember, they're the ones who assassinated Anwar Sadat when I was a year old!"

"Allah help us," said George.

"The Brotherhood is so anti-Semitic. They talk and say that the Jews today are not the same Jews that Allah had praised. They say these are the children who wouldn't listen to Mohammad when he taught us about Allah. They say

Allah was angry with them and turned them into monkeys and pigs." Vick took out a cigarette and lit it.

"Yes, I've heard some of the members talk in the coffee shop. They talk about the end of the world when the Muslims will fight the Jews and kill them all. It's this Qaradawi who talks so much about it from Egypt. He's a big shot of the Muslim Brotherhood," George answered.

Next Year 2010

"Ahmed, why do you torture the boy so much about his Jewish heritage from his mother?" questioned George, Nola's father. He was Turkish, born in 1925 and had arrived in Damascus in 1947 to open up a slaughter house, something his family had done for years. That meant that Nola was Turkish, too, even though her mother was a Damascan Syrian, and could cook some mighty delicious Turkish meals. One thing their family never had to worry about was not having enough lamb in the house for dinners. George's attitude towards Jews remained a little different from his Syrian friends and relatives. He wasn't that gung ho on hating anyone.

"George, I listened to Morsi, who is the head of the Muslim Brotherhood's politics today. He spoke on the TV. He said we must nurse our children and our grandchildren on hatred for Jews. He said they were Draculas and Vampires. He's telling Egyptians that their children must feed on hatred. Hatred for them must continue everywhere! The hatred for Zionists must go on for God and it's a form of worshiping God! I agree with him! He's a smart guy. He should be president of Egypt!".

"Nonsense. This is the year of 2010. That crap went out with Gamal Nasser. Listen. Just because Israel has a blockade of Gaza now is no reason to call them all the names he has. Phew! Do you know that those guys have been bombing Israel's South since 2001? It was time Israel did something big to stop it. How can they live like that?" retorted George.

"That's the point, George. They shouldn't live," shot back Ahmed.

Anti-Semitism in Sweden was highlighted in the city of Malmo. 2010 saw Muslim immigrants there make up 20% of the city of 290,000 or about 58,000. It is also a city where Jewish Holocaust survivors had been living peacefully since the 1940's.

Judith Popinski was rescued from a Nazi concentration camp and was able to go to Malmo where she lived for sixty years in peace, raising her family. The Swedish people had treated her with great kindness, and all was well until the town had a new mayor who wasn't Swedish nor did he care for the seven hundred Jews. In 2009 The Muslim immigrants set the Jewish chapel on fire. They've desecrated the cemeteries. Orthodox Jewish men were abused on the way home from the synagogue.

They have been not only harassing Jews living there but have been going around with loudspeakers blasting "Sieg Heil" and "Hitler, Hitler." They threw rocks and bottles at Jews they saw peacefully demonstrating in support of Israel. Vick laid down the magazine after reading about Sweden, then continued to read. March 15, 2011 "Syrian Civil War Started" was the new article he read next.

"It looks like a lot of Iraqis have moved to Sweden," mentioned Vick casually to George one afternoon after coming in from work. He put down his construction crew hat and hung up his jacket.

"Yeah." George smiled. "I guess they like all those gorgeous blondes. I bet you do, too, Vic. Are you thinking of visiting Sweden someday? Ha! I thought you liked redheads!"

FOUR

January 2012

Vick worked at Khayyat Contracting and Trading from 2000 to 2012. He was a manager in this major Italian Investment and Development Company in the Syrian industrial project referred to as the "Steel Melt Project." It had given him experience in how to deal with a large number of people at the same time who were all from different counties, backgrounds and religions. Working also with some small contracting companies broadened his experience and made him more valuable to the company. He was able to write a safety code for the government as an OSHA system evaluator. Vick had become a man of substance and importance.

"Things are not looking up, Nola," called out Vick from his computer. He just read that the Syrian government troops had stormed the village of Basatin al-Hawawiya which was on the outskirts of Homs. The report was that 106 civilians had been killed. This happened on the 15th of the new month of the new year of 2012. "What a way to start the year!" he fretted.

In his reading, he stumbled onto the "**Damascus Affair**" in which Jews were again accused of ritual murder. It was back in 1840 in Damascus. Finally he had a chance to see what had ticked off the average Syrian towards Jews. He never could understand this hatred that they felt. He came to feel that 1840 was a calamatous year all around the globe.

1840, that was when Glasgow, Scotland had so many cases of typhus, typhoid and relapsing fever and didn't know how to cure them or how they came to be. Neil Arnott, a physician in 1840, had said that the great mass of fever cases happened in the low windy and dirty narrow streets and courts where lodging was the cheapest and where the poorest and most destitute naturally lived. From one place between Argyll Street and the river, 754 cases out of 5,000 of fever that happened the year before were carried to the hospitals.

Vick started to think of what it must be like to live in the poorest sections of Cairo and Syria and wondered if they had such fever attacks today. Two years before, in 1838, the entire Jewish community in Meshed, Persia were forcibly converted to Islam. That same year was when the Cherokee Indians in the USA were forcefully removed from their homes in the SE part of the USA and moved to Oklahoma on the "Trail of Tears" when 4,000 died in the winter. Then he went on to read that William Henry Harrison won the 1840 presidential election and defeated the incumbent, Martin Van Buren in that year in the United States. He wasn't familiar with these names exactly. There was an autonomous government called Oregon Country in 1845, an Oregon Territory by 1848, and the state of Oregon was created in 1859. Thus, a lot of pioneers were moving out to Oregon in covered wagons when the Jews of Damascus were up for the blood libel. Then he started reading about the Jewish tale of Damascus in 1840 and wondered if his maternal ancestors were involved. What an era of time that was! Were his Jewish ancestors even here in 1840?

It was on February 5, 1840, that the Capuchin friar Thomas, an Italian who had lived a long time in Damascus, had disappeared with his Muslim servant, Ibrahim Amara. Vick thought that because he could speak some Italian, he might have found out what had happened if he were back in 1840. Not any Syrians spoke Italian like he did that he knew of. How stupid to think that Jews used human blood. He thought he could have done a much better job of talking to them in their own language before the fiar had disappeared. Italian is such a beautiful language, he thought.

Though Friar Thomas was a monk, he was involved in some shady kind of business, and the truth must have been that they had been murdered by tradesmen during a quarrel. The Capuchins were gossiping to their friends that the Jews had murdered both men, and of course that was more believable to the anti-Semitic neighborhood. They believed that they had been murdered for their blood for the Passover matzos.

At that time, Catholics were in Syria under the French protection. An investigation would have been carried out by the French consul, but the consul, Ratti-Menton, allied himself with the accusers and supervised the investigation together with the governor-general, Sherit Padia. They were barbarous about it. The barber, Solomon Negrin, was arrested and tortured until they got a confession out of him. They made him say that the monk had been killed in the house of David Harari by seven Jews. He had to name them so they knew who to arrest. Two of them died under torture. One was converted to Islam in order to be spared. The others were made to "confess." A Muslim servant working for David Harari told under pressure that Ibrahim Amara was killed in the house of Meier Farhi. Meier saw it happen and so did some other Jews. They were all arrested, but one, Isaac Levi Picciotto, was an Austrian citizen and under the protection of the Austrian consul, so Austria, England and the United States intervened for him.

Then they found some bones in a sewer in the Jewish quarter and the accusers insisted they were the bones of Thomas and buried them. The tombstone read that it was the grave of a saint tortured by the Jews. Then more bones were found, said to belong to Ibrahim Amara. Dr. Lograso, a well-known physician, refused to certify that they were of a human and asked that they be sent to a European university for examination. The French consul wouldn't okay the request. The authorities were adamant that because of the confessions and the remains found, the guilt of the Jews in the double murder was proved beyond a doubt. They also grabbed sixty-three Jewish children to force them to tell the hiding place of the victims' blood from their mothers.

The whole Jewish world became alarmed at this Damascus Affair. From Alexandria, Egypt came a petition to Muhammad Ali because of Israel Bak, the Jerusalem printer. The Austrian consul general in Egypt, A. Laurin, was sent a report from the consul in Damascus and also sent a petition to Muhammad Ali to stop the torture methods that had been used on the Jews. Thus, torture finally came to an end on April 25, 1840. The investigation against the Jews continued, though. Even Rothschild was brought in to intervene with the French government but didn't help. James de Rothschild, without the authorization from Vienna, sent a report to the press. His brother, Solomon Rothschild, went to the higher ups with the result that an order was sent to Damascus on May 3, 1840 asking for protection for the Jews from the violence of Muslim and Christian mobs.

Western Jews were shocked at what had happened in Damascus and Jews in France and Britain saw it as a sign of the Dark Ages returning. It alarmed the assimilated Jews, such as Lasalle, who had completely broken away from Judaism. Non-Jews who were enlightened and educated also protested against the accusation through the press and at mass meetings a Jewish delegation got together including Moses Montefiore and others who left for Egypt to meet with Muhammad Ali. They asked that the investigation be abandoned and transferred to Alexandria for judicial clarification or be considered by European judges. Because war was imminent between Egypt and Turkey, the request was not granted. The Jews decided to let it go with the liberation of the prisoners without the declaration of innocence. That came out on August 28, 1840 and the prisoners were saved.

Montefiore wasn't finished with the affair, though. He went to Constantinople with his delegation where they appealed to the sultan to publish the *firman* which would proclaim blood libels fallacious and prohibit the trial of Jews on the basis of such accusations.

Yet, the Catholics of Damascus continued to tell tourists for many years about the saint who had been tortured and murdered by the Jews and how the Jews were saved from the gallows by the intrigues of Jewish notables from abroad. This event made the Jews of Damascus aware like they never had been before, since the Spanish Inquisition of 1492, of the need for intercommunal cooperation which led to establishing the Alliance Israelite Universelle. In other words, they learned that Jews everywhere needed to unite in order to save themselves.

This even was accepted as true by the press in Europe. Stories came out in April saying that the body of Father Thomas was suspended head down and one of the Jews held a tub and collected the blood while two others applied pressure to make the blood flow faster. Then, when he stopped bleeding, they cut his body into pieces.

England wasn't quite as blood-thirsty in their reports, but "The Times" was against Judaism and said that the onus of disproving ritual murder fell on the Jews themselves. This all led to the publication of the Protocals of the Elders of Zion. In 1986, when Vick was only six years old, Mustafa Talas, the Syrian Minister of Defense, issued another edition of the protocals along with other documents from the case. This idea of ritual murder was charged over and over in the Arabic-language media and by diplomats from many Arab states. The tomb of Father Thomas's remains still stands in the Franciscan Terra Sancta Church in Damascus and carries the words that he was "murdered by the Jews on February 5, 1840."

No wonder that Assad treated Jews as violently as he had done. These descendants of the accused Jews had grown into their role of the frightened misfits, afraid to stand up for the barest of rights. That Vick came from a woman among them shows that once they were great fighters and leaders, too. Oh, what a "cross these Jews had to bear" for the past one hundred fifty-four years out of which Vick had been born.

Mike Wallace of the TV program, 60 Minutes, went to Syria in 1973, a year after the Yom Kippur War, and interviewed some of the 4,500 Jews in Syria. They had identity cards with MOSSAWI stamped on it in big red letters which meant, JEW in Arabic. However, when Wallace interviewed a pharmacist, the man was afraid to tell the truth in case of reprisal and said that they were treated well and what Mike had heard was simply Zionist propaganda. A school teacher said in her interview that she'd never be able to be friends with Israelis. Wallace's program bordered on the inaccurate and distorted facts about what was really going on in Damascus, Aleppo and Qamishi in their Jewish neighborhoods.

FIVE

February 2012

News on TV blared into the living room. "The Syrian Observatory for Human Rights have reported that sixty-eight bodies were found between the village of Ram al-enz and Ghajariyeh. Syrian activists blamed pro-government militia tonight, this date of February 27, 2012. This is being called the Ram al-Enz and Ghajaniyeh massacre. Ghajariyeh is near Homs.

"Things are getting bad," Alaa said to Yana when she was bringing him a dish of rice pudding she had made. "Be careful when you drive to your office. You may be a lawyer, but you're still a woman. Our government forces fighting rebels who want an Arab Spring to come here is dangerous for us all. I don't agree with it. It's getting so I'm worried about you driving at night."

"You're safe, my dear," retorted Yana. "Being the head of a TV station has its advantages. How'd you'd like tonight's newcast?"

"It was just okay," Alaa said, thinking of ways to jazz it up. He was angry that the whole truth couldn't be broadcast and had to be so careful as to how events were presented or he'd lose his head, most likely. Thinking of the freedom that the USA TV stations had made him wonder several times if there wasn't a need after all for an Arab Spring and a change of government but then, they had had it so good, too. Life had been quite easy. They didn't want for money.

March 2012

"Do we know anyone in Karm al-Zeitoun?" called out Vick at work from his office at KCT where he worked as an engineer.

Sara, his bookkeeper answered that she didn't think so. "Why?" she dared to ask her boss, the boss she loved but thought was really strict.

"The Syrian Army was reported to have massacred forty-seven people after they entered this place on the 9th of March. God! That was the day after my 32nd birthday! What a way to remember that!"

"Come on, Vick," called his friend, Elijah on his cell from outside in front of Vick's luxurious home. Let's go! I don't want to be late." The group of friends was going to see Sacha Baron Cohen's "The Dictator." They had heard it was terribly funny, and Vick didn't think that anyone had caught on that the main character was by a Jewish guy.

"Be there in a jiffy," he replied, and closed up his computer. He had just read about Sweden being so anti-Semitic. That was a shock to him that hatred for his mother's people carried over to Sweden, so far away. In the city of Malmo during a tennis match, they had had problems. The Israeli flag burning happened in Stockholm, the capital. Sweden was shifting their policy to favor Iran and Syria these days. The Swedish telecommunications giant, "Ericsson," has contracts with Assad's regime and they refused to be forced by the EU to cop out of their contracts with them. Tehran, Iran and Damascus, Syria used this technology to crack down on pro-democracy movements in their countries, but Sweden is putting money first.

"What are you doing in there?" continued Elijah.

"Dreaming of tall blonde Swedish girls," he answered wistfully. Yes, a nice tall viking girl would be so nice to dance with being he was six foot three inches tall. He heard they were quite sexy, too.

April 2012

"I hate to hear the news these days, Nola. Do we have to listen?" Vick asked in earnest.

"I want to know what my country is doing, Vick. We have to be prepared for the worst or for the best. I don't like to be in the dark."

"If things don't get better, it won't be long before we are sitting in the dark," he admitted.

The news came on. "Good evening, Syria. A battle occurred today on April 5th in Taftanaz, in the Idlib Governorate. Our army was reported to have carried out a massacre by rounding up and executing people after the Battle of Taftanaz. Sixty-two people were killed. Of course, the army denies executing them. They were simply killed in battle."

May 2012

Another massacre occurred in Houla on the 25th of this month. Forty-nine children were among the dead. The UN concluded that the Syrian government forces were responsible. This was followed up on the 31st with a massacre at Al-Buwalda and the al-Sharqiya massacre.

"That's all that's happening in this country; massacres in all the cities. Soon we'll be next for living near Yehuda Quarter," sobbed Nola. She could no longer defend Abbas as strongly as she used to, though they personally had reaped benefits from him in education and health.

Vick was in the middle of the Civil War of Syria in his town outside of Damascus in May of 2012 and couldn't believe what he was doing. With shaking hands he was going through his safe in his home office and taking out his money and passport.

It all had started on the 15th of March, 2011 with unrest, and then by April protests of demonstrating people were growing in the streets. The Syrian army was brought in to stop the uprising, resulting in soldier firing on the demonstrators as they were instructed to do so. It was the Arab Spring that was riling up the people. They decided they wanted President Bashar al-Assad to resign, and he wouldn't comply. The protests from the people turned into an armed rebellion and was made up of defected soldiers and civilians without any central leadership. It got so bad that Vick was afraid to drive his navy blue Mercedes Benz 180 C class to the site where he was starting a new apartment building. That development job would have to wait now.

His childhood home was right in Damascus, next to the Jewish quarter, Harat al-Yahoud. It was probably in danger, too, but was so big and beautiful. It looked indestructable. He hoped it would never be harmed.

Right now his stepmother and stepsisters and their families were waiting for him. Hurry, hurry. He quickly found his passport and money and damned be the rest. He would come back for essentials. He mused that he'd only be gone for a month at the most.

"Hurry, Uncle Vick!" wailed Zeinah, his niece. She was his favorite, always wanting to sit on his lap. He laughed mostly when his two nieces were with him. He loved children. Someday, he thought, he'd have five, but not with any of these Muslim women. He wouldn't have his children brought up with ideas like that. He already had picked out names for his first two; Adam and Eve. That's how much he loved to read about the beginning of the world.

Vick's religious education was from being exposed to Islam by his Muslim family of step-mother Nola and his three step-sisters being his father, Mohammad, had died when he was three years old from cancer. The extended family included his father's parents that he didn't care for and his step-mother's parents, George and Amalia that treated him like real grandparents should.

Vick had refused to go to the public Muslim grade school and begged Nola to let him attend the Catholic school, so she finally relented. He stayed there until high school, which he was forced to attend. From there he went to colleges in Damascus and in Beirut, Lebanon to become an engineer.

Some time ago while still in grade school, he had stolen into his late father's study, since Nola and the children still were able to live in it, and had found the old Masonic textbooks on a shelf that obviously had been his father's. He had the audacity and time to read from them. He wanted to know what his father saw in them and why he was a Free Mason. Luckily, he could read them because they were in English, a language he was quite fluent in from English classes in school. Between the two resources, he had formulated an idea about his Jewishness that his uncles had mocked him about because of having a Jewish mother. He had also found some scrolls written in Hebrew, the language of the Jews. Oh, how he'd like to be able to read those!

There was nothing he could find on Judaism in Syria so as to learn more about his mother's religion. All such subjects were forbidden along with the reading about anything from the Free Masons, who were what the Masonic Order was all about. It was a toss-up as to which was considered the worst. All the more reason why Vick wanted to know about them. His father was a Mason, he thought maybe a Master Mason. Nola said that he traveled around a lot because he was a bigshot with the Masons. He wanted to know about his father and was said to look like him. His father was brilliant. So he would be, also.

His projects. The mall he had overseen to be built. Would they stand up against all this fighting? An engineer with Khayyat Contracting and Trading Co., he had already seen to many projects that went up lately being he was the project manager. He had attended the American University of Beirut, or AUB. This schooling in Lebanon had brought him OSHA requirements of safety engineering, a plus for this young Syrian Muslim. The rest of his schooling had been at Damascus University. That's where he would take his family now. Back to Lebanon. They had to get out of Damascus because the fighting was getting too close.

He had rented a minibus that would hold everyone. Nola and Yana would be waiting with the children. He would drive them away from these missiles and get a house to hold them all in Lebanon where he had many friends, even his old girlfriend from college. Though he had studied health and safety environment at OSHA, an international school in Damascus and a part of Damascus U, he was now a safety engineer and had studied in Beirut where he met, dated and had a love affair with Brittney, a Christian Arab.

SIX

Lebanon

Vick, hurry up, we're hungry," whispered Yana, who was his lawyer and half sister. Ever since the stranger had come to his house and told him of his birth mother, Yana had been the only sister to protect him from the others in the family. His father's brothers were always making snotty remarks about his Jew mother. Could he help it if his father had fallen in love with a Jewess? Of course, that explained why he himself was always defending Jews, didn't it? That didn't go over well in his house except with his stepmother's parents. His grandfather was always defending him to the rest of the family and telling them to listen to him!

Listen, Ahmad! Listen to Vick! He's right in that Jews are not all bad. Why, my friend, the Shokhet in Yehudah Street was a wonderful man. He said prayers before he slit the throat of a calf. He did that so the calf wouldn't feel pain. We talked a great deal about the feelings of animals and how our role in life was to not only feed ourselves but to do it in respect to God. How can Vick know this and then spit on them like you do? He's smarter than all of you crazy Halabis! Maybe he does take after his mother! Good for him!" Vick had already parked his Mercedes in Amer's garage for safekeeping. He was his Lebanese Christian friend from college. Vic had rented a minibus in Damascus in order to bring those of his famiy who were leaving with him. Amer loved the idea of a Mercedes gracing his lovely garage.

Vick debarked out of the minibus carefully, his 6'3" frame bending so as not to hit his head. Muscles bulged as he picked up several suitcases at a time from his boxing years at college while his family jumped and tumbled out of the bus and ran up the steps and opened the door of the rented house of Vick's friend. They unpacked and set about to have something to eat. Luckily his mother had packed some food they could eat with their fingers. A pomegranate, some oranges and pears were in his stepmother's food basket along with a sack of those good pistachios from Aleppo and some walnuts. She had also packed some shawarma lamb from last night's dinner that they nibbled on. That went well with the pita she had wrapped up so carefully to keep fresh and soft.

He and Yana put the children to bed and Vick told them some bedtime stories of the genie who kept coming to him at bedtime. Vick was not telling a tale, he was telling about something he fully believed in; that he had a visiting genie in his ancient homestead. Not only that, but he saw many ghosts there. This genie was something special, though. He didn't tell the children, but he had sex with her many a time when she crept into his bed and lay on top of him. This engineer, who had a mathematical mind close to Einstein's, believed in ghosts and genies, and thought that his genie helped him on many occasions.

"So the genie crept into the cave and stole the bags of gold," he continued, and seeing that his charges had fallen asleep, yawned and crawled into another bed and fell asleep, dreaming of that beautiful genie friend of his and wondering if she would visit him that night while he was in Lebanon.

"No," he had insisted to Yana. "She's more than a wet dream. She's real!"

He thought of the ghost that kept coming and going out of his bedroom in Damascus. One time it had led him to the basement, where he followed, and saw that there was money buried in the floor in a box. Vick covered it back up thinking that someday he might look at it again.

He flipped on the news on his portable radio to catch up on his Syria. Here it was, the 22nd, and he heard that rebels claimed to have killed twenty-five men who they accused of being a part of the Shabbiha. This happened in Darat Azzah in Aleppo, and was called the Darat Azzeh massacre.

A week of this close living with his relatives were getting on Vick's nerves. He went over to his old girlfriend, Britney's house to relax and make his mind up as to what to do. Though they had been in college together in Beirut and that she was a Christian Lebanese, he wasn't seriously into her. She wasn't interested in his interests, only sex. The bombing was continuing and according to reports coming into Lebanon. This was 2012, and Assad's forces were holding off the rebels and both groups were causing damage in the neighborhoods. One couldn't tell who one's enemy was these days. Besides that, the rebels were affiliated with either al-Qaeda or Hezbollah from Lebanon, both terrorist groups. Vick was afraid that if he stayed in Syria much longer he would be drafted into the army. He wouldn't kill a snake, let alone a human, so he would refuse to become involved. This he couldn't do. He may be Syria's number one smuggler, but he wouldn't kill. He had his limits.

As they climbed into her bed, he noticed that she had slipped off all her clothes. Stark naked, his girl was devoid of any body hair anywhere except the long black hair from her head, her crowning glory. That's how he liked his women. He wore his Yves St. Lauent cologne that wafted into her nostrils and caused her to bend down and kiss him on his lips. He took her into his arms and showered her with kisses from her lips to her nipples that he bit gently, noticing how it grew in his mouth. They lay together enjoying the warmth of their bodies together. She grabbed his black hair and made love to him. They had been lovers before, and this was just like the olden days at college. Moaning and groaning, suddenly Vick let out a cry of relief at the same time as Britney. Vick fell back, finally drained of energy and felt so relaxed for the first time in many days. He was happy he had found a partner who had no plans to tie him down. They simply enjoyed each other and that was all there was to it. He took out a cigarette and lit up. Here it was the 30th of June 2012 and he was on his way to safety in Egypt. He and his mother and sister and nieces would fly there on Egypt Air.

June 2012

Vick wanted terribly to become a Mason, which his father had been. Vick believed that he had been a Grand Master. He found the website of Masonery and put in a request to join on the 5th of June that evening. An answer was not forthcoming. He looked fondly at his father's ring that he had been wearing since he was fourteen. "Someday," he thought.

On the 6th of June, eighty to one hundred people had been stabbed and shot in Al-Qubair in Maarzaf, Syria. It was figured to have been executed by the army of Syria, but then, they didn't go around stabbing people, did they? Vick guessed it was the rebels. He was only too anxious to leave.

After Vick and his family had landed in Cairo, by June 2012 President Assad told his government of Syria that they faced "real war" now, indicating the authorities' conviction that the fight would be long-lasting and it needed all their attention and they were to forget their old priorities on the table. They were to table everything else! The Halabi family felt they got out just in time.

Shortly after Vick and his family arrived in Cairo, they found an apartment to stay in at the May Fair Village in El Sherouk City, a suburb of Cairo. It advertised as a residential compound. It was nice, not as much room as they were used to, but it would do for now. It was something for them all to get used to when they listened to Egyptians speak. They spoke this harsh Arabic that the Halabi family considered hard on their ears. Maybe they could get used to it, but they hoped they wouldn't be around long enough to do that.

"Vick! Morsi is president! Here it is, June 30th, 2012 and he's become President Morsi! We won't have to worry now since it was him who made sure we could come here without all the visa problems," screamed Nola happily.

"Yes, Nola. Everything is going to work out just fine," commented Vick. "This calls for some Jack Daniels." Vick left the apartment in search of a liquor store in very Muslim Cairo, where the head of the political arm of the Muslim Brotherhood was just elected president. Little did he realize that there were going to be some changes in store for Egypt now.

"Nola, why did Morsi do that for us Syrians? Why did he allow us in so easily? What's in it for him?" searched Vick in his mind.

"Alaa thinks he wants us to owe him one, and that we'll vote for the Muslim Brotherhood party in the future, but of course we won't be here long enough to be voters," laughed Nola.

SEVEN

July 2012

Vick stayed up late searching on his computer. He was able to read so many more reports about Judaism and the rest of the world now that he was out of Syria. Assad kept a strong hand on his people. They couldn't get on the web like other people in other countries. Everything was censored. With the responsibility of getting the family out of Damascus came the agonizing worry about what was coming next. Vick couldn't fall asleep unless he had Fluffy on his chest, the little kitten he had taken from one of Nola's new friends whose mother cat had had kittens. This one was a charmer. Vick had insomnia. Usually he would fall asleep around 4:00 am, and then sleep until about 7:00 am. He was getting dark bags under his left eye, the one that had been injured from the beating he had taken back in Syria's prison. He could no longer see out of that eye as well.

"The weather is warm, just right in Taba," reported Vick's new Egyptian friend, Omar. Let's go there and do a little deep sea fishing and diving. You said you go down 150 feet?"

"Yeah, but how far is it from here?"

"It's about 215 miles. I'll drive. We can make it in three hours, easy. Want to go?"

"Are you kidding? Of course," answered Vick eagerly to have a chance to go diving, a sport he loved.

"Meet you tomorrow morning, 5:00 am. Be ready then, I'll honk," directed Omar.

Bright an early, Vick managed to get all of two hours sleep, and he was ready and dressed. They drove the three hours with the radio on blasting away Egyptian belly dance music. It put Vick to sleep, and he caught up on the third most important hour of sleep he needed.

"We're here!" exclaimed Omar.

The two went into the office and registered and paid a fee for their equipment. A guide went with them to the boat. They went out and first did some fishing. Then they both jumped in and sunk down. Taba was near the northern tip of the Gulf of Aqaba and was the busiest border town crossing with neighboring Israel. It really was a little more than a hole in the wall where a bus used to come with a luxury hotel that even had a casino. It's the most favorite spot for Egyptians and tourists, especially those from Israel on their way to other places in Egypt or as a weekend party city. They call this city, "Egypt's Riviera."

"This used to be in Israel's hands in 1956," commented Vick. Israel returned it to Egypt in 1957 when they withdrew and then they reoccupied it again and the whole Sinai Peninsula after the Six Day War in 1967. That's when they built the 400-room hotel. After the 1973 Yom Kippur War, Israel claimed that Taba had been on the Ottoman side of a border and been in error and they returned most of the Sinai in 1982 and Taba was the last piece returned to Egypt in 1989. We might even meet some Israelis here because part of the agreement was that Israelis could cross from Israel to Eilat at the Taba border crossing and visit visa free for fourteen days. Taba is a very popular tourist town."

"Look at the hotels here, Vick, cried Omar. Which would you like to stay in, the Hyatt Regency, Mariott, Sofitel or Intercontinental.

"Of course, the Marriott," said Vick jokingly, but did you know that in October of 2004, the Hilton Taba was hit by a bomb that killed thirty-four people including Israeli vacationers? The bombers were said to have had help by the Bedouins on the peninsula.

"Well, we don't have to worry, do we. We're not staying overnight in a hotel. We can sleep in the car if we have to. Now, we can either go free diving or scuba diving. They even offer classes in diving here. If that gets boring, look, over there, see?" Omar pointed to the right towards the desert. See that?"

"Oh my gosh! A desert style golf course! Ha!" I wonder who put that in, the Israelis or the Egyptians!" wondered Vick.

Later, while they were in the sea, a small shark could be seen out of the corner of Vick's right eye. He didn't panic. He loved all animals and had no fear of any of them, even sharks. He really thought he was indestructable, but then he had a wonderful awe of all life and would not harm any of it. They saw all sorts of small and large colorful fish. Vick could have stayed down forever, he thought. He loved to explore in the depths. As he came up, he noticed another boat close by and immediately spotted a black-haired hot chick that looked quite tall standing in the boat in her diving attire. She looked like she had just come up and had taken off her head covering. Black hair fell down to her bottom. "Wow," he thought. "Who is she?"

He and Omar went over to some folding chairs when they got out of the water and sat down, tired from their swimming, and ordered a Turkish coffee from the waiter who came over to them. Vick noticed that the other party on the boat next to theirs was also standing in line getting some orange sodas. The girl picked hers up, walked over to the chairs, and sat right down next to Vick!

"Salaam," she said in Arabic. "May I sit here?" she continued in English, hoping he would understand.

"Of course, please do," Vick answered in English, much to her pleasure.

She smiled. "I'm Aviva," she said.

"Aviva. Where do you live?"

"I'm from Tel Aviv," she replied, looking into his brown eyes watching for a reaction.

"Ah," answered Vick, grinning. "I'm Jewish, too!" he declared openly and happily. The thought of a Jewish girl from Israel elated him immensely.

"Do you come here often?" she asked, puzzled to find another Jew in Taba, thinking that he had to live in Israel, then, but noticing that he didn't answer her in Hebrew. Omar didn't understand any of the English the two were speaking. He left them to look at the magazine stand.

"No, this is my first time." he answered.

"Where do you live?" she inquired.

"I now live in Cairo," he responded. "I'm actually from Damascus."

"A Jew from Damascus? How interesting. I didn't know any still lived there," she added.

"I guess I was one of the last to live there, and now I'm the only Jew living in Egypt," he said, "except for a few old ladies who take care of one of the synagogues. No other men, just me. I've only been living in Cairo for a short while and haven't met any yet."

"Have you gone to the synagogue?"

"Yes, and it looks deserted to me. It wasn't open." reported Vick.

"If you go there on a Saturday morning, it might be," she answered, looking at him quizzically.

"Thanks, I'll have to try it again," Vick said with a sigh, thinking of the traffic and how long it took to get there. Little did either of these two young Jews realize that orthodox Judaism expects one to walk to a synagogue on Shabbat. They were to live close enough to be able to do that.

"Wanta take a walk with me?" asked Vick. Aviva looked up at him and smiled.

Vick took her hand and they walked around the docks and looked at the ships mooring there. Finally they walked behind a lot of stacked up boxes waiting to be aboard some ship, and looked around. The rest of their friends could not see them. Vick was standing close to Aviva, and gave her a quick kiss to test her reaction. She in turn put her arm around him and gave him a much better one that lasted longer. Their mouths opened and Vick's tongue searched the inside of hers. Then they embraced closer and Aviv could feel a swelling above his hips right in the center of his torso.

"My God, but you taste good," he said.

"You too," she replied, and she stepped out of her shorts. Vick took the cue and undid her bra and quickly stepped out of his shorts. They stood there against the boxes and made love, with Aviva's legs wrapped around his body, clinging to him. It was over in a flash. Both had been as hot as firecrackers.

"Good afternoon, Vick," dug Nola. "Welcome to the living."

"What's new?"

"Well, Mohamad Morsi issued a decree calling back the parliament that had been dissolved." she reported.

"Oh oh, a fight already. I can smell it coming," he suggested.

"Maybe. He has called for new elections to be held within sixty days of adopting a new constitution." she said.

"I bet it will be rejected by Egypt. Morsi had no right to reconvene this parliament after the court ordered it dissolved in June." wagered Vick.

"Yes, well, they now have until the 24th of September to finish drafting their new constitution," said Nola. Maybe you should join them in writing one. You've got so many ideas in that head of yours."

"Thank you, Nola."

"I'm going to take a trip up the Nile with some of the neighbors," Nola told Vick. "Would you like to go with us? It should be fun."

"Thanks, Nola, but I'm going to see if I can get some work. See you later."

"Remember, Vick. Ramadan starts on the 20th. I won't be eating until sundown until it's over on August 19th. You'll have to make your own meals during the day if you want to eat. Just please don't cook on the stove and make me smell good food. Wait till I cook something. Then you can also."

"Good lord! That was something I didn't have to worry about living in my own home," he replied.

"Ramadan. Oh my God! How you people can go all day without eating is beyond me."

"You get used to it, my dear. I've been doing it all my life." Nola retorted.

August 2012

"What's happening in Syria?" Nola asked Yana. She longed to hear from her friends in Damascus, but they didn't all have computers.

"I heard that there was another siege of Hama where one hundred or two hundred people were killed. They say it was the Syrian government forces again who did the killing when they held an assault on Hama. It had started on the 31st of July and just ended on the 4th, she said

"Yeah," piped up Vick, who had walked into the room and joned them. I was in Hama several times. It's where all the Muslim Brotherhood brothers hang out and plot more Sharia Laws to try to enforce on Syrians. It's one hundred and twenty-two miles away from Damascus. Do you know what the four largest cities of Syria are, Yana?" Vick loved to quiz his family on facts, something so easy for him to remember with his photographic memory.

"Aleppo, Damascus, and I think the third is Homs," answered Yana, who was a lawyer and had been doing quite well.

"What's the fourth?" teased Vick.

"I don't remember," gave up Nola.

"Hama," he replied.

"Nola, don't you remember when we visited the water gardens?"

"They dated back to 1100 BCE," commented Yana. "I loved seeing that place. Those poor people"

"Poor my eye," retorted Nola. "It is the center of Assad's enemies, the anti-Ba'ath groups. Back in 1964 they were raided during the Islamic Uprising."

"Yes, and when I was a year old, 25,000 people were killed there. It is referred to as the Hama Massacre of April 1981-82," threw back Vick as he brushed his hair with his long fingers.

More news blared on the TV on the 25th. Many people were killed in this five day army assault on the town of Darayya, Rif Dimashq, which was being held by the rebels. According to the opposition, Human Right Watch and some local people, they said that the killings were committed by the Syrian military and the Shabiha militiamen. When the government was questioned by the TV station, the massacres were committed by rebel forces. So local residents backed up their claim.

October 2012

"Sixty-five people have been executed, allegedley by the Syrian Army," commenced the TV newscaster. "This number includes fifty soldiers of the Syrian Army who were defectors. This massacre at Maarrat Al-Nu'man was over in six days, from October 8th to the 13th.

Sweden was the first country to offer help to the Syrian refugees in 2012 and took in 8,000 refugees. They offered them permanent residency besides. They could bring their families.

"Maybe we should have opted for Sweden instead of Egypt," remarked Vick teasingly to Nola. He knew that logistically, Egypt was the best place for his step-mother so that she could be closer to her three daughters as well.

"So what's Israel doing with all this going on?" she asked. Vick replied, "They're actually in Jordan to help the Syrians. They're helping the children and infants who were injured by our government crackdown. Other volunteer groups have aid in the refugee camps in Turkey and Jordan. Syrians that have crossed the border into Israel have been able to get medical help. Their hospital in Safed has treated many Syrians already. Too bad I didn't cross into the Golan and get help for my eye. After all, I got it in our lovely prison when I was picked up.".

November 2012

By August, President Assad was being asked to resign by the UN General Assembly who came up with such a resolution. The USA's president Obama warned that using chemical weapons would tilt the USA towards intervention for sure. There had been rumors that it was being used.

"Nola," called Vick from the TV. "Come see this! The major opposition forces of Assad are uniting and are calling themselves The National Coalition for Syrian Revolutionary and Opposition Forces. The Syrian National Council are joining them. They're meeting in Qatar, of course, where they will have their comforts. I guess the Council didn't want to be left out of the fun."

"Listen, Vick. The Islamist militias in Aleppo and the Al-Nusra and Al-Tawhid groups are refusing to join the Coalition. They just said it was a conspiracy! Damn them! Here it is, November 2012, and they're divided. We'll never get back to Damascus at this rate.! We've been here almost six months already. I want my kitchen. I want my garden. How can I cook without my own herbs!" Nola broke down and cried a little.

The next month, the USA joined Britain, France, Turkey and the Gulf states in formally accepting the National Coalition as the legitimate representative of the Syrian people. Adieu, Assad. Jordan's refugee camp, Zaatari, a camp for just Syrians, was now official by December 2012.

December 2012

"Is dinner ready yet?" called out Nola to Vick, who was the cook tonight. He was grilling lamb chops outside in the garden, a pretty expensive meat here in Egypt, and smashed potatoes. Vick hated rice and refused to cook it. A salad would round this off with some pastry he had bought.

They had had his lentil soup for lunch, and it had been delicious. Vick loved to cook. He used all fresh ingredients, and would buy no processed foods in the market.

Even the meat back home had to be fresh. Vick went to the chicken farm and would pick out his hen himself and watch while they slaughtered it to make sure it was done correctly. The same process happened with his lamb. He didn't trust the markets.

Nola had been next door visiting the neighbors, also people from Damascus. She turned on the news on the TV set.

"Morsi signed the decree today, Wednesday, December 26, 2012, which will be a day to go down into the history books," said the commentator. "This puts Morsi's constitution into law. It had reached the final approval stage, though many felt it was ambiguous, they passed it. The vote was ten million for and six million against it. Congratulations, Egypt!

"Dinner's ready," called out Vick. "Some constitution," he thought to himself. He now kept his thoughts to himself these days since he realized that Nola and he weren't on the same page about Morsi. "How can he trust such a guy who was so against Jews," he thought. Every day Vick had been meeting people in the stores or in the coffee shops, mostly, who were so outspoken against Jews. He would question them and finally get them to see where their thinking was quite off key. He spoke with such authority and such a beautiful way of speaking Arabic that before they knew it, Vick had charmed them into agreement, and they would leave smiling, glad to have run into such a wise person. He had opened their minds. Occasionally he would run into a stubborn fellow, not ready to listen at all, who would just pronounce the usual shpiel against Jews.

December wound up with Assad's Alawite villagers being killed by Syrian rebels. Ten were confirmed killed. This happened on the 11th of December in Aqrab, a Hama Governorate with actually one hundred twenty-five dead and wounded counted in the melee.

EIGHT

January 2013

Friday the 25th was a day of violence in Cairo as tens of thousands came out to demonstrate in Tahrir Square on this 2nd anniversary of the revolution. Seven protestors and two police officers were killed in clashes in Suez, the state media reported.

"Listen," said Vick to Osama, a friend who had joined him in watching TV and playing Sheshbesh to pass the time. "More than two hundred fifty people have been injured in other battles around the government buildings all over Egypt. Boy, we want to avoid those places like the plague. It's not safe to walk outside anymore. Aren't you glad we live in the suburbs?"

Osama answered by reminding Vick that they had seen the military with their armored vehicles in Suez on their trip there by bus to look for jobs. The Muslim Brotherhood offices had been ransacked and burned in Ismalia, where they had gone. They were lucky to escape without being arrested.

In Cairo, masked men had attacked the Muslim Brotherhood offices. They had smashed their computers besides the regular vandalism of turning over the furniture and spreading broken glass on the floor. These attackers were not the military but came in a large group and carried pellets and acid to burn the padlocks with, and they stole the computer hard drives. It was a planned attack.

"Osama, these Muslim Brotherhood people have dominated the elections since the president was deposed. Look at what Morsi did. He overruled the authority of the judiciary so he could make sure that his Islamist allies could push through an Islamist-backed constitution to referendum over the other parties' objections as well as that of the Coptic Church," lectured Vick.

"Yeah, the Egyptians will never let the Muslim Brotherhood rule. Morsi got the Presidential Palace and the blame for all the problems that Egypt has," answered Osama.

"The revolution had brought on two years of turmoil. Thank you Mr. Obama, for churning up this state which was to be our refuge from our turmoil," said Vick." "People go to Tahrir Squarre because their demands of bread, freedom and social justice have not been met."

"Did you see the banners now in Tahrir Square? They are saying that the Brotherhood Constitution should fall."

"Everyone is a dreamer," interrupted Nola who just walked in. "Reality is still the same, here or in Damascus, so different than all of our dreams." She had picked up a poster that read, "Injustice, the guard of our lives." It was unjust that the rebels ruined her happy life in Damascus where she was just getting started as a fashion designer. Who could think of designing clothes now in such turmoil? She was getting tired of wearing the same old clothes she had brought with her and she didn't dare spend money buying anything new. She had to save it for flying away. How could she make anything with her sewing machine back in Damascus. She wondered if the house had been hit by any rockets, yet. "Allah, keep it safe," she prayed.

February 2013

It was Vick's turn to cook again today. He decided on Tabbouleh, which would take him only a half hour to fix. He had the bulgar wheat, two large tomatoes, parsley, some fresh mint leaves which he had growing in his herb garden back in Syria and was lucky to find here, he thought. Oh, how he loved to use mint. He also had a red onion, lemons, sea salt and some olive oil. He would grill the flatbread to go with it, for Nola and her neighbor friend were coming to join him for lunch. Then they would drink some Turkish coffee afterwards and visit. God, he had to keep busy doing something. He remembered how they would keep a pantry full of food enough for a year at a time back home in Syria. Everyone did that. The only people he has learned that do such a thing were the Mormons in the United States. His family, or rather Nola's family had been doing this forever, he was told. Otherwise he could walk to the neighborhood market for certain items they would run out of. There was nothing of this going to the supermarket every week for Vick.

Another nice touch was that in Syria they had a milkman who deliverred milk in glass bottles every day. He loved whole milk and drank a lot of it. It was second best to drinking Scotch, he laughed to himself. Muslims may not imbibe, but he did on occasion, especially with the Americans that he would meet.

Gerta was coming over pretty soon. She was coming over to play Sheshbesh with Vick and to see Fluffy, his cat. She was in the neighborhood visiting some friends. He had to get ready.

Gerta walked in and saw that Vick was all alone. "Where is your step-mother?" she inquired.

"Out for the day on a trip," replied Vick as he put his arm around her and pulled her close to him, giving her a kiss on her lips.

"I don't have a lot of time," she warned. Gerta was a German girl who was working in Cairo that Vick had met in the coffee house. He spoke some French, since he was from Syria, and it had been under the French mandate after the Ottoman Empire had fallen, and he spoke some Russian, but he didn't speak any German, so they conversed in English.

"Okay then, let's get down to business." He beckoned her to his room, and she started to take off her clothes. With her arm up over her head, Vick saw that she had tons of arm pit hair, and he freaked out!

"Gerta, stop,!" But it was too late. Gerta looked at him as she was stark naked, and wondered why he said, "Stop!"

"What's wrong? Is someone coming?" she tittered.

Vick couldn't tell her that he would not, could not make love to a girl as hairy as she was. A razor had never touched her body. She had hairy arms and hairy legs and a huge mound of hair between her legs. It made him gag to look at her naked as she was.

"Yes, I saw a taxi cruise by with Nola in it, I think. I'm afraid you'll have to leave now. Sorry," Vick said, givng up the opportunity for a quickie. Here's the money for fare. Get dressed quickly and go!"

Gerta ran out the door, quite astonished. She didn't see any cab, but called for one on her cell phone as she stood under a palm tree. Having dieted for the past week and losing three pounds, she thought that was a wasted effort and wished that Nola hadn't gone by.

March 2013

"Vick, please go with me to see the Cairo International Fair." A few of my friends here from Damascus and I want to go, but we want a man to go with us. We're a little afraid to go on our own. Please, Vick. You'll enjoy it," pleaded Nola.

Vick thought a minute and decided to do it. Heck, he might like to see what Cairo had to offer in the line of females who would also be attending, he hoped. "Okay, Nola. Tell your friends we'll all go. I'll rent a big taxi for us. The center must be about twenty miles from here."

"Egypt is so much larger than Syria. They have at least one hundred twenty million people. We have only about twenty-two million, so this fair should be fantastic! But I'm a little afraid of large crowds," Nola answered.

"Nola, Cairo has over nine million people alone! That's why I can't get a job. They have too many people and not enough jobs for all, exclaimed Vick. He got up and got himself a glass of water out of the water cooler in the corner. They didn't dare drink water out of the tap as it came out in a brown color, like it looked in the Nile River.

"My God! Damascus has about five and a half million people. It's our second largest city," Nola told Vick after looking it up on google. "Why, Cairo is almost twice as large.!"

Maybe you'll get some fashion ideas like burkas," laughed Vick. Old Morsi really is trying to go into a religious Sharia type of era, back about two hundred years or so," he chuckled. "Nola, your modern styles will not go over well in this country at all!"

"Shalom, Ari," wrote Vick to one of his Jewish friends on his facebook message page. "I want to learn more about Judaism. What can you recommend that you like to read?"

"I have just the thing for you, my friend, typed back Ari. "Have you heard of Kabbalah? I'm sending you four parts of Sepher Yetzirah. Enjoy!"

Vick had not read any of the Torah or any Tanakh. He had studied the New Testament in his Catholic grade school, and the Koran, and here he was commencing to read Kabbalah, which was something meant for only men of the age of forty and older who had studied Torah as a prerequisite. Ari probably didn't realize this either. So many people had heard that Madonna was reading the Kabbala that many American Jews thought it was just a rage to read it it and that everyone could understand it.

"Every element has its source from a higher form, and all things have their common origin from the Word (Logos), the Holy spirit, so G-d is at once, Spirit in the highest sense, both the matter and the form of the universe. Yet He is not only that form, for nothing can or does exist outside of Himself; His substance is the foundation of all, and all things bear His imprint and are symbols of His intelligence."

Vick read for three hours before he stopped for a bite of dinner. He was eating this stuff up, and understanding it. His joy was in ideas, not daily goings on in Syria or Egypt. He thrived on ideas.

In college he had made some money writing papers for his friends who had no time to study. He made sure their papers got them a good grade, and he loved studying other subjects other than just only what he was signed up for. If there was a project to be made, it was right up his alley, as he was an engineer in his mind and heart before he even finished all his studies. He knew how to create. Vick remembered something once he read it, so there was no late-night cramming needed for him. Facts were there in his mind. He made a bundle off other college students.

Nola came into Vick's bedroom and woke him up. "Vick! Yana's friend was just killed! It was horrible!"

Vick opened his eyes and looked at Nola. "Who was it? Anyone I know?

"I doubt it. It happened pretty close to the house, though, in Damascus."

"My God. What happened, Nola."

"It happened during evening prayers at the Sunni mosque on Frieday the 22nd and Sheikh Mohammad Said Ramadan al-Buti was leading the prayer service when a suicide bomber from Al'Qaeda hit. Yana's friend was killed with many others there."

"Why did they decide to hit a mosque? Al Qaeda is very Muslim. They're hitting their own kind!"

"He was a supporter of President Bashar Assad, like I am. Oh my God!" wailed Nola.

They turned the news on and the commentator finally got around to mentioning the attack in Damascus. Assad was vowing to purge Syria of extremists now that they had attacked the mosque he had frequented many a time.

"Yana is back in her home in Syria, and had called me to tell me about it. I wonder if our home is in one piece," cried Nola. That was her greeting of Welcome Home. The children are wondering why she is crying so much today, she told me."

The news on TV went on. Israel has just apologized to Turkey over the Gaza Flotilla deaths that occurred after they had bordered the Turkish ship.

"I bet Israel will have to pay a lot of baksheesh for that apology," commented Vick. "They never should have apologized to the Turks. They had every right to board that ship," Vick said in a louder than usual voice. "You can't deal with people unless you're stronger than they are."

"Barack Hussein Obama is visiting Israel and the West Bank and is winding up his short trip today," reported the news commentator, about to end the program. Barack is an Arabic name which the Swahili language also has adopted. He's named after his father, who was the senior Obama. President Obama was a great admirerer of his father," and that wound up the nightly news.

"I wonder if he's also a Muslim," asked Nola.

"Not according to what he tells us," answered Vick. "He says he became a Christian when he married Michelle. He may have been before that, though. Many Blacks in America have become Muslims, so I've heard. He would have never been elected president if he had been a Muslim. I don't like that man," commented Vick. "I think his father, back in

Africa, had been one for a period of time, though. But then he became a Christian."

"Oh my God! Look what I just read from the New York Times from my computer. Last year a bomb dropped near this man, Darwish's house from our Syrian military plane so he got a shovel and went into the olive grove near his house and dug through the sealed entrance to an abandoned Roman cave," repeated Vick.

"Where did this happen?" asked Nola.

"The cave is one of many in Sarjehin, Idlib Province," Vick explained. "The Civil War has been going on for almost three years now, and Assad is having neighborhoods that are aligned with the rebels hit. So this Darwish fellow and his family have been living in this damp cave, and have been joined by their neighbors. It's all up in the northwest part of Syria. Look, it says that his fifteen year old son has carved the word "HOME" in Arabic above the cave's door. Oh my God!"

"How can they live in caves? asked Nola.

"Grimly", replied Vick. "It says here they have a routine of eating, keeping warm and dry, gathering firewood and water and all the while they keep their ears open to listen for planes and artillery shells. These caves may have been used as pens for livestock once."

"Living in a pig sty, most likely, only none of us eat from pigs. The Romans probably did, though," answered Nola.

"People used them to live in during the days before Jesus while they were building a nicer home, some think. Today these families like them because they have nice thick walls. The villagers are saying that tens of thousands of people are living in the caves," answered Vick.

"I found such a cave once," recalled Fouad, a neighbor who had been standing outside at the screen door and had been listening after nearing the door. Nola let him in and he sat down across from Vick. He had come to visit with Nola.

"I did, too," added Vick, thinking he was the only one who had ever found them. He always thought that would be a great place to stash some of the things he smuggled in the old days. A Sheikh family was said to be living in a smaller cave farther up the hill from the Darwish family. Sheikh said he couldn't live in the village anymore, so he had spent thirty-five days of working on his cave and making it habitable. He put in a wood-burning box stove, cut a ventilation hole, dug and took away mud, hung up heavy blankets to get rid of drafts, and made a nice warm corner for his living room.

His family was a typical Syrian family where neatness was next to Godliness. This warm room is kept very neat and shoes are stacked at the edge by the door. He keeps it well organized. Now that they lasted through the cold winter, his wife has swollen legs. Their three small children have chest infections and earaches. He's lost twenty-five members of his family from the shelling already. He was afraid that even his cave family wouldn't live through all the shelling.

"How did the cavemen ever survive under such conditions?" Fouad asked.

"Maybe they were made out of tougher stuff than we are," concluded Vick. "Or maybe they had a lot of children and only a few made it to adulthood."

One thing the cave people had to contend with more than home living people of today were bugs. Bugs would permeate the cave easily and had to be flicked away. Vick thought of this as he got up and looked for the fly swatter, found it and smashed a few flies.

"Ahem, what did they do in lieu of a bathroom? I'm afraid to ask about this," inquired Nola.

"The article says that on up the hill from the caves, rocks had been stacked to form the walls of a small outhouse. They used a blanket to hang as its door and this hid an open trench they had dug." said Vick.

"Isn't that something! I read about Roman soldiers once, and each of them carried a shovel with them so they could dig out a toilet and cover it up again," reported Fouad, who also loved to read about everything, especially about the ancient Roman days.

"Let me see that article," said Nola as Vick handed it to her. She scanned and then read aloud to the group. "One lady was pregnant and only left the cave to go to an aid station to deliver her baby. They had built the baby a tiny hammock in the cave. From another cave farther up, one could see a rope that had laundry draped over it in the open air. Some caves were stocked with hanging kerosene lamps, blankets and bedrolls which were places much safer than their own homes."

"I could never live this way," moaned Vick who loved his own home that he had decorated with all imported utilities. He wanted the best, the state of the art luxury that the world had to offer. "If he couldn't live in the USA, he brought the USA to him in this way," he told Nola.

Nola blamed the UN and the West for doing little to help Syrians. By withholding weapons from the opposition and sending only limited aid, they are in essence collaborating with Iran, Russia and China in the destruction of Syria.

"What kind of friend is the West when they invite Syria to the Friends of Syria Conferences of the French and Americans that lead this? They are supporters of the Syrian opposition. What kind of friends are they, anyway? Backstabbing friends?" she told them.

NINE

April 2013

Becoming more adept in writing in English gave Vick the nerve to join in on a discussion about making peace between Muslims and Israelis on facebook. It was led by a beautiful Turkish woman and was discussing the merits of believing a very controversial Turkish man, Adan Aknar, who was a TV personality. Vick was defending him. Adan had done a 180 degree turn around towards Jews and many found it was hard to believe him. Vick commented that they were all striving for a better future and all wanted peace, but now they had to work for that peace. He thought that the Muslims' offer of friendship on facebook with the Jews and Israelis should be taken seriously and they should not be condemned by taking them as fakes. He said that we would know by the end of the road whether they really meant it or not and it would be a good start for others, but if we crucify the Turkish leader of this discussion group, no one would ever dare to step on this road from the Muslim's side. He noted that we needed friends.

Then Vick let it be known who he was, a Syrian Jew who had fled to Egypt. He had suffered, losing much of his family and home, so he had tried to enter his beloved Israel to live with his people and had been rejected. He felt he had been treated like the enemy. Even when he had added friends from Israel on facebook, they unfriended him as soon as they knew that he was from Syria! He said to the group, "I'm Jewish, for crying out loud and they refused me!" He was deeply hurt by this rejection of so many when all the time Israel and Jews had meant so much to him.

"So," he went on, "It's not the Muslims. It's everyone not from Israel that should say that they were wrong in order to maintain a friendship."

He then went on in another post. "I just wanna say I'm very truly sorry if I offended you in any way, but I think that u and me are on the same team and I'm not the enemy. I simply speak another language. Sorry again. I didn't expect u would block me for nothing."

So much misunderstanding happens through language and especially through writing, even when one is writing in one's own native language.

"Good evening from Damascus. The battle of Jdaidet al Fadi has continued since the 16th till tonight, the 21st with a hundred dead. Our Syrian army was accused by the opposition to be carrying on a massacre. SOHR claimed that two hundred fifty people were killed since the start of the battle. They say they have documented by name one hundred twenty-seven of the dead which includes twenty-seven rebels. Another opposition group is claiming that four hundred fifty have died. In Rif Dimashq an activist claimed he counted ninety-eight bodies in the streets and eighty-six in the clinics who had been executed. Yet another activist said that they documented eighty-five people who were executed. This included twenty-eight who were killed outright in a makeshift hospital."

"Everyone is considered an activist," suggested Vick. "I can't stand this news. I have no country anymore. It's being overrun with foreigners and everyone else is dying!"

"It's all the Jews fault, Vick. You don't want to hear it, but it's true. Don't give me that evil eye!" threatened Nola.

"I've read facts, Nola, since I've been able to use the web here in Egypt. Half of the Jews of Aleppo had to flee in December 1947 even before Israel was announced as a state by the UN. Seventy-five Jews died in that pogrom. Don't give me that old wives tale that it's always the Jews' fault."

"They're at the root of everything. They're always riling up people and getting them to do things," she retorted. "Let me see what I can find on google. Here's something you missed. The Aleppo Artillery School was the scene of another massacre on June 16, 1979 where thirty-two to eighty-three were killed. They were probably Jews, too," shouted Nola at Vick.

"I've also found out that the year I was born, 1980, was the year that Aleppo was under siege and more than two thousand died then from many massacres over quite a span of time. Then the next year in April was the Hama massacre where four hundred died. The men in Hama were rounded up and executed. Some free state we're living in. I was lucky to not be living there and was only a year old," he admonished. "All my life, Syria has been killing off its own people."

"I remember Hama, all right." Look it up in google and see what it says," coaxed Fouad. "Hama, February 1982, ten-thousand to forty-thousand died. Another Hama massacre where two thousand more died happened after those others," he added.

"What was going on in Hama?" Vick wondered aloud. "Hmmm, here's something else. There was a Tadmor Prison massacre on June 27, 1980 that I missed seeing. Palmyra had five hundred to one thousand massacred in that prison."

"That keeps everyone towing the mark," explained Nola. "If they step over the line, they get massacred. We don't fool around in Syria."

May 2013

Syria was still in turmoil. On the 2nd and 3rd of May, the Alawite militias held an assault against the local Sunni population and killed anywhere from one hundred twenty-eight to four hundred fifty people. This was in Bayda and Baniyas, the Tartus Governorate. Vick had held no ill will with Assad, the head of the Alawites. In fact, he had admired him for being a doctor.

Vick woke up with a jerk as his cat, Fluffy, was on top of his chest agaian and beside him was his laptop. What thoughts kept creeping into his head from when he first left Lebanon with his large family and when his step-mother and he had flown to Cairo. Here he was in a gated community outside the largest city of Egypt where it was incessantly hot day and night- no change, hot permeated into your pores, your shower, your tea. It was 2:00 am. He would sleep for a few hours and then get up for the day. Starting off with a glass of warm water and a little cider vinegar added to it, Vick checked his page in facebook. Then he managed to have a cup of Turkish coffee and a couple of eggs and an orange. Even a former boxer had to keep in shape, and he was a strong disciplinarian about his eating habits. Everything had to be fresh.

He checked his messages on facebook again. His computer was getting worn out, he feared, as he used it so much for work. He had become most interested in Jewish friends and the things they posted. He started posting Jewish comments as well, identifying with them. He even chose a very Jewish background for his wall of the march of Jews in Rome of 70 CE. He announced to the world that he was Jewish, now that he learned that by having a Jewish mother made him Jewish, too, even though he knew very little about being one, other than everybody hated them. Good, this fighter would fight for their rights!

Here it was, May 2013. He learned on Cairo's TV news that Hezbollah had entered the war in support of the Syrian army. Russia was also sending support. Vick could speak some Russian being Russians were a common sight in Syria. He had many occasions to speak with them and practice, especially with the gals.

Iran was also the one sending money into Syria. Qatar and Saudi Arabia were transferring weapons to the rebels who were fighting the army. Everyone was getting in on the act!

"Deborah, can you find out something about my mother for me? Asked Vick in May of 2013. "Could she have gone to Israel in 1994 in some group?"

Deborah was his pen pal on facebook, a friend that he started to ask questions from since she was an American and an Israeli with dual citizenship. She was another of those people who posted good things about Israel on facebook. Besides that, she wrote a lot in her blogs she had started to post there as well, and Vick had been reading some of the pieces.

Deborah later told him that a Judith Feld Carr had led out most of the remaining Syrian Jews in 1992 and 1994 and had taken them to Israel via the USA and Europe. She was from Canada and also a mother of six children. Her neighbor had told her that she had lost a daughter in Auschwitz and had said, "You can never let this happen again to the Jewish people!" These words led Judith to become a human rights activist.

Vick thought about all the things he had seen in his father's house that could bring in some money. He still knew of a few treasures and wondered what they were worth. He had taken pictures of them and brought them up from his picture file.

"Deborah," he called on Skype. "Look at these pictures. I'll post them on message. Go back, you won't lose me. They'll come up in a minute."

"Here they are," Deborah said excitedly. "How beautiful! How did you come by these?"

"They've been on the shelf in my father's study. Do you think they're worth a lot? Can you find out for me?" implored Vick. "They might be worth enough to buy me a visa to Sweden. I need about $5,000 to get one"

"You have to BUY a visa?" asked Deborah suspiciously.

"Everything costs today, Deborah," Vick said matter of factly. Vick thought that he could always fly back to Syria and retrieve these two pieces if they were worth the trip and then some. He had in mind that the two might bring in at least $50,000. They were gold, heavy, and he thought they went back quite a few generations. No telling how his father had them in his possession.

TEN

June 2013

The Syrian rebels turned on Shiite villages today, June 11th, and killed thirty of them. This happened in Hatla, deir el-Zour, Syria and is called the Hatla massacre. Yana saw this in her mind as a whole large class of first graders being slaughtered.

"What are the rebels doing killing off civilians?" she asked her husband. Alaa was speechless. He couldn't fathom why.

"Aarf, aarf, aarf," bellowed a dog from somewhere in Faroh City near Vick's apartment. It had been barking all night, not allowing him to get the few hours sleep he needed, since he was unable to sleep most of the time.

"I'm going to do something about this poor dog," he told Nora in the morning. "I don't think any of us are sleeping these days with that poor dog crying day and night."

"What's going on? Aren't they feeding him?"

"I don't know, but a dog doesn't bark without a good reason," put in Vick.

After breakfast of two eggs and an orange, Vick walked out in his garden and listened. "Arf, aaarf," bewailed a very sad dog.

Vick started walking toward the sound and it wasn't long till he found the origin. Just two apartments away, another ground floor apartment had a dog chained up outside in the sun, and Vick noticed that it had no water dish. He was infuriated.

Ri..ng, ri..ng. Vick rang the doorbell and a rather short and stocky older man appeared. "Hello, sir," said Vick in a rather sullen voice. "Is that your dog outside?"

"Yes, it is," the man retorted in a rather official manner, as if nothing was wrong by having a dog outside.

"It's been keeping the whole neighborhood awake every night, and I'm tired of it," stated Vick firmly.

"So!"

"I'm asking you to do something about it. I don't like to see a dog treated that way!"

"Get off my property, you twerp! Do you know who I am? You don't come barging over here telling me what to do!" The neighbor screamed at him and attempted to close the screen door.

Vick let out one punch to the nose of this jerk with his long arm and the puffed up official, whoever he was, could have been the mayor of Faroh City for that matter, landed flat on his back.

With that good deed done, Vick strolled out to the yard, and undid the chain around the dog's neck. He called over a boy he knew from the neighborhood that he saw standing nearby and told him to take the dog to the police station which was nearby so they could find him a good home, and he gave the boy the equivalent of $36 to do the deed, which was 250.84 Egyptian pounds (EGP).

Out from around the corner came a couple of thugs and the neighbor who was shouting and pointing at Vick. Vick stood up straight and tall, showing off his height of

6'3" which made him almost a foot taller than the three approaching him.

"Sir," said a bystander who had come out of his apartment, "do you know who that man is?"

"A jerk," answered Vick. "A jerk who has no sense of taking care of a dog, who doesn't mind torturing one."

"That sir, is the head of the Muslim Brotherhood here in Faroh City. Those two others are his bodyguards."

"Where is my dog!" questioned the offender of dog rights as he saw the chain but not his dog.

"He went to find another person to take care of," Vick answered. "He said he was not going to live with you anymore, and you were lucky he wasn't going to sue you for negligence."

The two bodyguards had to look up at Vick to see that his eyes were covered with sunglasses, and he had a cigarette in his hand that was busy wiping off some sweat. They looked at each other, nodded, and poked their boss in the ribs, and they all turned around and went back into their apartment.

Later, a trio of older men with beards rang Vick's bell. Vick opened it up, and the men politely asked if they could come in.

"Mister Vick," they said to him. "We are the Committee of Peace here in Faroh City. We don't call the police over spats between neighbors, but we would like to help you make amends with your neighbor."

"Hmmm, just like in Damascus," Vick said. "We had the same system in the neighborhood where I lived.

"Good. We have been talking with the other neighbors, and they are cheering you on for taking care of the nuisance of the dog barking and keeping everyone awake every night. To them you are a hero. They were also so happy that you knocked him out. He has been lording his position over everyone and terrorizing them. Being most of us are refugees from Damascus, we all share this fear of being sent back to the killing fields of our homeland."

"So, what do you want from me?" asked Vick.

"Come with us to his apartment. We are going to ask you to shake hands with him and get him to forgive you."

"That'll be the day," said Vick.

"It will be right now," the committee cajolled. "Come with us. Then we will have something nice to eat."

The four of them walked over to the Muslim Brotherhood leader's home and rang the doorbell.

He answered, a man who now was greeting them with a taped-up nose.

"Ah, the man I wanted to sue!" he blustered. "You're lucky the Committee of Peace interceded. I was going to sue you, but luckily my nose isn't broken after all. You see, I also am an eye, ear and nose doctor."

"All right," spoke up the leader of the committee. "We want you both to shake hands and apologize." Vick and the doctor extended their right hands and shook, and then they put their arm around each other and gave a little hug. Then out of the kichen came the wives of these men with cakes and Turkish coffees already in little cups on a tray. They all sat down and commenced visiting.

"You know, I want my dog back," said the doctor to Vick.

"No you don't." Vick answered strongly. He doesn't want you."

Vick told Deborah all about it the next day. "Deborah, we had a system like this in my neighborhood in Damascus. We never had to call the police over neighborhood fights," he boasted."

"How did you do that?" she inquired.

"One family, one man in the neighborhood, the richest of all the people, was the head man. Any dispute between people, and he was called in to be the arbitrator. He decided who was right and who was wrong, just like King Solomon."

"Or, like the Godfather!" exclaimed Deborah.

"Yes, and after the two shook hands, then the head man would take the whole neighborhood to the restaurant and they'd have a party in the banquet room."

"My gosh, and who picked up the tab?"

"He would. That's why he had to be rich," laughed Vick.

"Well, if it works, it works," she giggled. "They don't have to pay taxes to the government for so many policemen that way. Cool!"

"Too bad we don't have anything like that here," she said sadly, thinking of the pioneer days and that maybe they had something going like that on "Little House on the Prairie."

"Why not?" You mean you call the police if two guys punch it out?" Vick asked.

"Well, we didn't all grow up together in 300 year old houses that are fenced in with high walls like in Mexico City, and we come and go a lot, so we don't know our neighbors. Sometimes we don't even go to the same schools. Nobody would stand out to be the Godfather unless maybe he was a psychologist. Nobody here would take the responsibility or would be afraid of being sued. No, it's a lost cause here."

The next night Vick brought up the subject of psychologists. "We don't have psychologists here in Syria. That's silly."

"Why, there's lots of reasons why people need to see them." Deborah answered.

"If you have a broken arm, you go to a doctor, but not for thinking," he commented. Changing the subject, Vick brought up living in Los Angeles. "I would love to see that city," he said, "and Philadelphia too, so that I could see the Liberty Bell there."

Somehow they got on the subject of homosexuality. "I think it's all wrong!" he exclaimed. It's against God's law."

"Vick, that's something they can't help. They're born that way."

"Not in my city, they won't be," he emphasized.

ELEVEN

July 2013

On July 3, Mohammad Morsi was deposed from office. The world was calling this a coup. The military was taking over the reigns of the government of Egypt. He was the man who had invited the Syrians to come to Egypt in his aim of collecting more votes for the Muslim Brotherhood's party.

The military started to think of ways that could get rid of so many unwelcome guests. Egypt already had enough poor to bother with. They didn't need more on their hands. Not at this time.

After coming back home from work, which he did mostly on his computer, Vick had bad news by the middle of July 2013. The owner of his apartment, a lawyer at that, wanted Vick to clear out of the house by the first of August because the lease was not in his name! On top of that unsteadying shock was the fact that the Egyptian government was trying to reduce the number of Syrians in Egypt. Since they hadn't needed a visa to enter Egypt with, all those without a residence card were to be deported and that meant Vick.

"Good Lord, I am one of 300,000 Syrians here," thought Vick, "and only 125,000 are registered. Can Egypt force us to leave?"

Egypt was busy coercing many to do just that, but the UN had reminded them that they couldn't legally do such a thing. Even so, they managed to detain more than 1,500. Living in Faroh City had its advantages. They were in the suburbs, away from the central part of Cairo and all the rioting.

Vick had been picked up and questioned and held overnight without any food for being an Israeli spy after first arriving in Cairo. How they came up with that, Vick wondered. Was it because of websites he had put on facebook, he wondered? He used an alias there. How could they know? Being his passport showed he was a Muslim from Syria, they had no proof and finally let him go. He was getting to be an old hand in police stations, he felt.

July 2013, and Syria's army had taken control over about 40% of the country's land and 60% of the Syrians themselves. Back in 2012 the UN had called this fight as "overly sectarian" in nature between Alawaite shabiha militias and other Sh'ia groups fighting against Sunni-dominated rebels. Everyone denied whatever was said.

A knock at the door and Vick opened it to find two policemen there. "Come with us," they half whispered, looking around inside the apartment. Vick patted Fluffy and followed them out. "Not again," he thought.

He was ushered into a sparse room at the police station and asked a few questions. "What is your name?" He answered, "Amram Halabi."

"Let me see your passport," remarked the Chief of Police in a stern voice.

"Hmmm, Muslim, from Syria. Where is your residence card?"

"I don't have one, sir. I tried to register, but they weren't registering anymore of us."

"You realize that you cannot stay past December 31ˢᵗ. Then you willll be removed," the chief remarked.

"Yes sir. By then, the war should be over and we'll be back in Syria before that."

"You have been reported to be an Israeli spy. You might be out of this room far faster and into our prison if it checks out, Amram. Follow Sergeant Mohamed. You now go into a cell while I check this accusation out." directed the Chief.

Having been taken so early, with just finished his water with vinegar, Vick hungrily followed the policeman and was thankful it was a lone cell and not a room for torture that he was taken to. He laid down on the cot and fell asleep. Twenty-four hours later he was released. They could find nothing on his laptop or his phone, and there was no record of him spying. He was glad to get back home, grabbed the bottle of milk and gulped it down. Man, was he hungry. All that time without any food.

Vick ate his fill, and did the dishes. He then took his laptop that the police had confisgated but gave back to him, and rechecked it to make sure nothing had been deleted. Then he sent a message to Deborah, his friend.

"Deborah, how r u?" he typed out carefully. I'm sorry I didn't write yesterday. I was in jail for being an Israeli spy. I want to go to Israel! Can you help me? Please, I must get out of here and find Liliane."

On July 15, 2013, Deborah got a letter out by e-mail to a friend working for the "Forward" who was pretty well known. She told him briefly about Vick and the necessity of getting this last Jew out of Egypt and into Israel. She told him that he was studying Hebrew by himself and said that since the law said that you are Jewish if your mother is, he has every right to feel he is Jewish and has been on the side of the Jews his whole life. She went on to say that he could help Israel in so many ways, and told him to check him out himself on facebook.

On July 22nd, Deborah wrote to the "Consulate General of Israel Embassy" begging for a chance for Vick to get into Israel to live, and that he was afraid of reprisal for being Jewish and living in Egypt. If he is sent back to Syria, which they threaten to do to these refugees, chances are he'll be killed because of some informer of his being Jewish. His lease was to be up by August the 1st and he might be deported then.

The former Chief Rabbi of Syria, Rabbi Abraham Hamra, was now living outside of Tel Aviv. Deborah wrote to him on July 28th and told him of this son of a Jewish Damscus Syrian woman that he may or may not have known about. However, there was the chance that he saw to his bris when he was circumcised.

Vick had told her of the time when at the age of five or so, he and a little girlfriend, whose mother had come to visit his mother, were playing under the sheets and she saw his noonoo.

"Oh," she cried out. "Yours doesn't look like Basem and Azado's. Is it okay? Does it hurt you?"

Vick got out of bed immediately and ran to his mother, screaming, "Mama, mama, I have something wrong with my noonoo!"

His friend thought that was a sign that he had been circumcized, most likely at eight days by Liliane, proof that he had a Jewish mother, when most Muslims circumcized their boys at age 13 years. What Deborah didn't realize was that it didn't matter anymore when it was done and could be done in a hospital shortly sometime after birth or any other time by Muslims without much fanfarae, like in the Jewish society.

Deborah went on to say that she hoped the rabbi might know of a Liliane from Damascus and be able to tell them her maiden name so that he could make Aliyah. There was a time back when Vick was born in 1980, that people from Israel could be tourists in Egypt and bus to and fro, but not today. Today they were barely able to keep up the peace agreement that Sadat had made with Israel.

The Syrian refugees are constantly reminded that they could be deported back to Syria at anytime now, and Deborah was sure that Liliane was in the 1994 group who were said to have gone to either Tel Aviv or Brooklyn, New York. The rabbi could be saving a life if he checked. The only problem, thought Deborah, was that she was writing in English, and there was a good chance that the rabbi didn't read or speak English.

"How presumptive we are," she thought, "that everyone in the world understood English." She had gotten the rabbi's address from another Israeli friend who took the time to look it up for her in the telephone directory.

"Please don't be an old adddress," she said to herself.

Nola was living with Vick in his apartment and commented to him one morning, "Good Lord, more than 100,000 had already died in Syria. In June, thousands, some of their friends, possibly, were in prison."

Suddenly, before Vick could answer, her cell phone rang and Nola quickly answered, hoping to hear from her daughter, still in Syria, the younger one, the lawyer, Yana. It was Yana.

"What? $10,000?" Vick!" Nola screamed for her step-son. "They have Alaa in jail. How can they do that to him? He's head of the TV station!"

Vick took the phone from Nola and spoke to his sister. "Pay the ransom," Vick instructed. "Or they'll beat him to death. Remember, I've been there. I can't see out of my left eye anymore, Yana. Do as I say. Get the money and pay them off!"

Vick comforted Nola as they both sobbed in each other's arms, a rare experience for both. This brought back Vick's memories of what he had witnessed when it was his turn to be in prison and no one bailed him out, but left him there to die.

On the 22nd of July, the news reported that the Syrian rebels had executed fifty-one POWs in Khan al-Assal, Aleppo.

"What kind of war is this?" questioned Vick when he heard that POWs had been killed. Even the Germans didn't do that in the 2nd World War. So now the Syrians are even worse!"

"Nope," replied Yana, who had looked it up in her law book. "Nations vary in their dedication to following these laws, and historically the treatment of POWs has varied greatly. During the 20th century, Imperial Japan and Nazi Germany's attitude toward their Russian POWs were notorious for atrocities against prisoners during World War II. The German military used the Soviet Union's refusal to sign the Geneva Convention as a reason for not providing the necessities of life to the Russian POWs; and the Soviets similarly killed Axis prisoners or used them as slave labor. North Korean and North and South Vietnamese forces routinely killed or mistreated prisoners taken during those conflicts," she read aloud to Vick.

"God, that means that we haven't advanced even an iota since then in emotions," said Vick, shaking his head.

Yana wondered if any of the POWs were anyone she might have known.

TWELVE

Still a Hot July

Still, he hadn't given up completely. Here was an opportunity to do what he had yearned for for so long. A site to learn Hebrew! He signed up for that and saw it was not too difficult. Soon he was posting lessons for others from the site. Having a photographic memory as keen as his helped, and he had no problem remembering the new words. Periodically he posted "Free Mason" material as well. He could not let his father down without posting all the pictures he was finding of his father's favorite passion, other than women, that was. His visiting stranger had told him of his amours in Denmark, and that he might have more step-brothers and sisters there as well.

There was that new friend, Deborah, an American Israeli who wrote a lot of articles and posted on facebook. She had information about what Judaism was all about. Hmm, they're not really expansionists like the Muslims thought? He'd change that when he became a Jewish leader. They'd get back Judah, Samaria, and Jordan itself if he had anything to do with it. But Deborah said they couldn't. They didn't want Jordan. He'd have to talk to her about that.

He had a Jewish mother, Liliane. What was she like? The stranger told him that his father and she had married and that they were madly in love with each other. He had given her an antique Star of David to wear around her neck on a gold chain. Her father was a dealer in diamonds and knew good stones. The Star of David was a simple gold star that she loved, not too ostentatious. After all, she couldn't be seen outside her home wearing it.

"She had hazel eyes, Vick," the stranger had remembered, closing his eyes to see her face in his mind. "She had full lips and when I saw her, she was very well dressed. You know, expensive clothes, like a model. She looked sexy."

Vick thanked him for coming and telling him the truth about his life. So his birthday was actually sometime before March 8, 1980. That made him a little older than he had thought.

"Thanks, now I know they had their first disagreement over me as to where I would be registered," Vick laughed. "So my father didn't want a Jew on my birth certificate and had to get Nola to sign." Thank goodness she did, or I wouldn't have been born, legally!" he mused.

Jews had been forbidden to be in the downtown area of Damascus. They weren't allowed to travel more than three kilometers without a permit. The persecution of the 2,500-year-old Jewish community of Aleppo and Damascus started shortly after 1947. If they tried to leave they faced either the death penalty or imprisonment at hard labor. Jews couldn't work for the government or banks. They couldn't even get a telephone much less use one. Driver's licenses were not issued to Jews. They couldn't even buy property anymore. Jewish bank accounts were frozen. A

Jewish cemetery turned into an airport road which they paved over. Jewish schools were closed and handed over to Muslims. Before the Jews managed to leave with Judith Feld Carr in 1992-94, the secret police grabbed ten Jews on suspicion of violating their emigration and travel laws and for planning to escape and taking unauthorized trips outside of Syria. Those who were finally released reported being tortured while in the prison and seeing some terrible things happening in there. In November 1989, the government promised to let five-hundred single Jewish women to emigrate because they outnumbered the Jewish men there and could not find husbands, but only twenty-four were allowed to leave in 1989 and another twenty in 1991. Vick wondered if his mother was in one of these groups and had left before the 1994 group the friend had reported to him about.

Two people had disappeared after being jailed for traveling to Israel in 1987. Finally in 1989 they were given permission to contact their families. They had been sentenced to six years and eight months in jail in 1987. Two of four Syrian Jews were arrested in 1990 while trying to travel to Turkey without permission and were released the next year. The Jews in Syria continued to live in terrible fear as the Jewish quarter in Damascus was under constant surveillance of the secret police.

They were everywhere; at synagogue services, weddings, bar-mitzvahs and any other gathering where Jews might congregate. If they tried to contact any foreigner, that conversation was monitored. The American State Department reported that Jews are the only minority in Syria whose passports and identity cards note their religion and thus have to undergo a more thorough surveillance than the rest of the Syrians.

Jews had to have permission to sell a car or a house. All their letters or any type of correspondence was censored. They were not allowed to work in the public sector and many university programs were closed to them. If they wanted to travel abroad and were given permission to do so, a rare occurrence, they first had to put up a bond of anywhere from $300 to $1,000 along with family members who were actually held as hostages. This was also done in China at one time.

There was Alois Brunner, the chief aide to Adolf Eichmann who lived in Syria and acted as an advisor to the Assad regime. He had the protection of the Syrian security service, which reflects on Syria's attitude towards Jews.

Vick realized after reading about how Jews had been so treated that his mother's neighborhood on Yehuda "Jew" Street so close by to his father's home was really a ghetto. His mother couldn't leave on her own or she would have been hunted down and killed or tortured and raped. That had happened ten years before Vick had been born and a good ten years after his birth.

There had been twelve Jewish teen-agers who were trying to escape from Qamishli in 1970 and had stepped onto a minefield which had not only killed them but their bodies had been mutilated from the blast. Vick knew all too well how they were looked upon and defiled. After reading the Bible in class, he had defended all Jews, even the ones in his home town. How could the people of Moses, a prophet in Islam, be so hated.

He remembered the story of a man in Damascus who was talking about how Israel was the one who was responsible for the extinction of many Syrian grapes. They were said to be ruining the Syrian economy! The man went on to say that the Mossad had sent some kind of pre-genetic engineered wasps to destroy the grape fields. "Ha," he thought. "Jews were blamed for everything. You could count on them to be the cause, no matter what. Even if there was no rain, his paternal grandmother would say, "It's the old rabbis who hold the rain only for them! They do it by Black Magic! Vick thought to himself that we would never stop hearing such amusing stories from the Arabs and the rest of the Muslims.

And to have found out at the age of twenty-five that his mother was only his step-mother and that his real mother was Jewish was the biggest but most relieving shock of his life! What had happened to her? Why didn't she come back for him?

The stranger told him that Liliane went to Israel in 1994, as he remembered. Judith and her husband, Dr. Ronald Feld, wound up rescuing 3,228 Syrian Jews all in secret. It started with one phone call to Syria and led her to a life of the next twenty-eight years made up of rescue work and intrigue, turning her into some sort of James Bond. She had to rescue many people out of prisons and deal with the Syrian secret police. That's how she came into contact with Rabbi Abraham Hamra, the Chief Rabbi of Syria, when he was a young man.

Then Dr. Feld died in 1973 of a heart attack, but Judith didn't stop their mutual work for long. She later married Donald Carr who also wanted to get involved in rescuing these Jews. They spoke with a man in Israel who had been a prisoner in Aleppo for four years who was constantly under torture there. He had been told that his mother was dead, but Judith found out otherwise and reunited the two.

Her work didn't come to an end until September 11, 2001, otherwise known as 9/11, an hour before the World Trade Center fell. She had been saving rare Jewish religious articles like the famous Damascus Codex which was known as the Keter or Crown, written in the 12th Century in Italy that had been found in Damascus.

Because of this seemingly impossible task she had taken on and had succeeded in it, which met cutting through a lot of red tape, Judith was given many awards. Some were from Israel and others from Canada, her home. Like Moses, she had led Jews out of a land that had turned against them, but this time it was Syria. She was told by the Syrian government not to take them to Israel, so many got there by a round about route, and many went straight to Brooklyn, New York. Which way had Liliane gone? Neither the rabbi nor Judith could come up with a Liliane Unknown last name. All the people were listed by last names in their record books.

THIRTEEN

August 2013

"Vick," called Deborah. The USA State Department said they'd admit 2,000 Syrian refugees. I just heard about a man in Ohio who has a brother who is a doctor in Syria, and he's been trying to bring him and his family here. They're just a little older than you."

"I heard, too," Vick chimed in. "The USA had only taken in ninety Syrians since the Civil War began. I had looked into it when I was trying to decide where I should go."

"In August, the U.S. State Department said the U.S. would admit 2,000 Syrian refugees. Larry Bartlett, Director of Refugee Resettlement at the State Department told "America Tonight" that this 2,000 number will be shared among several different countries. He called it a "humanitarian gesture."

After countless calls and three voice-mail messages, someone at the State Department finally picked up this man's phone call. Asked if this made him optimistic, the American Syrian brother replied, "Not really, but at least somebody answered me this time."

Deborah had resorted to calling her Oregon Senator, Ron Wyden for help and was also told that to get here on a work visa, which was the only kind he could see that Vick would be eligible for, he would have to be some outstanding scientist that was badly needed here. That he was only an engineer made him in competition with all the other engineers out of work looking for a job in the USA. We were in a recession and everyone was out of work. The business would have to fill out all the papers for him to come after they hired him, and the whole process would take a little over a year. Vick didn't have the means to keep going for another year. He needed out and a job right now ASAP. She threw in the fact that he was a Jew living in a Muslim country and was in danger, but that didn't help matters either. Claiming political asylum from Syria was not working unless he got in as one of the few that would be accepted as a refugee, and now he wasn't even living in Syria! The only good thing she learned was that because he wasn't listed as a refugee, he was a little freer. Once you're listed in that catagory, the UN doesn't want you moving about.

For the refugees who are granted refugee status, the process can take over a year. For the Syrian in Ohio's brother, the only other option is a family reunification visa which can take up to twelve years.

One thing Deborah could say was that Senator Wyden did eventually notify Deborah about her e-mail inquiry and his secretary had called her on the phone and told her to call anytime about him.

Vick thought that this was all wrong. His sister, also a lawyer, had told him that it was possible to claim political asylum and enter the USA. Deborah was to contact an immigration lawyer on the East Coast. She thought that maybe the West Coast lawyers knew nothing about immigration of Syrians. She couldn't believe this. Then again, she was failing at contacting her lawyer contacts on the East Coast, too. If she had been able to contact her peer in New York, she would have told her that the USA had brought in almost 60,000 immigrants from around the world in 2012, but out of that number on 31 were Syrians.

The USA had used about $1.4 billion dollars for the Civil War, most likely in supplying the people inside Syria or in camps and communities in countries bordering Syria. This money was listed under humanitarian efforts for Syrians over a nearly three-year period of Civil War. The end result for refugees was that only fifty people were granted refuge in the USA from Syria in 2013. Altogether, one can say that about ninety people were able to enter the USA as Syrian refugees.

Lying there in the sweltering heat, Vick remembered how he got this garden apartment outside of Cairo in the first place. He had met a Russian gal in a coffee shop and they got together that night. While in bed, he asked if he could be her roommate since his mother had flown to Dubai to be with another of his stepsisters and he was alone. He was running short of his cash. She already had a boyfriend, she had said, back in Russia, but thought it would be okay. Besides, she had thought to herself, "he's so handsome." It would be nice to have a protector in the house. Maybe a lover as well. She had a good job but was getting a little lonely.

One day she ventured out of the apartment and joined a group of rioters in the streets near Tahrir Square. Somehow, she became the victim of attackers and came back with a badly injured leg. Vick had studied First Aid as part of his safety courses and nursed her back to health. Then she left and went back to Russia, leaving him with the apartment with a paid-up lease for six months. Vick led a charmed life. Somehow, women always were there to get him out of a jam. He was very lucky as this was a lovely apartment and the rent was 4,000 EGP or about $574.per month. This was a gift such as the geni would have brought to him.

He lucked out in being able to secure a job as a programmer nearby, but these riots were making it impossible to get there, or for his boss to get clients, for that matter. Finally he got word that the business was not opening up again. It was done for. Vick was forced to see that no money was going to be coming in, and his own was dwindling since this job was bringing in the money that was going out.

What did Liliane look like? Where was his mother now? Thought of her remained in his head. He had been told that she had to leave Vick with his Muslim father, Mohammad, when Vick was about ten months old. Why? How could a mother nurse a child and when he was about to walk, leave him? Was she disappointed with him? The stranger said he had heard that she went to Tel Aviv in 1994. He was already fourteen years old then. It would have been nice to have had a loving mother. What a life he was leading at fourteen.

By fifteen he had his own checking account. He was a man and the best smuggler in Damascus, even making out with the girls in school. What a hustler he had turned out to be. By eighteen he had banked $75,000. At nineteen he was smuggling five million dollars at a time. One time he carried $50 million dollars in the trunk of a car in 1998 and paid off the police captain with a bottle Scotch and a Havana cigar, a Coreba. He had his own $300,000 home. They had lived well on one of his father's pieces of property that had a stable, horses and a swimming pool. Thank God that his father had invested in property! Now Vick bought alligator shoes and drank Jack Daniels.

The stranger, who was this man? Vick couldn't recall his name, but remembered that he worked in the petroleum field drilling for oil and had worked in Syria, Iraq and Jordan. Was his name Issam? Was he Danish? Vick had been hit with such earth-shaking news of his birth that he didn't think to write anything down about the stranger who was the bearing of this sweet shock.

Time to get up already. After three hours of sleep, it was time to report to work. Oh no! He had forgotten. He had no job. He had been making 3,000 EGP or $430.56 per month after taxes, that that didn't cover his overhead at all anyway. He was also using his savings from Syria. By early on in 2013, money was now very important as Vick was not a refugee listed with the UN. He had come at the beckoning of Morsi, Egypt's new Muslim Brotherhood president. There was a reason why Morsi encouraged so many Syrian refugees to immigrate to Egypt. He had thought that they would be of the same mind-set as Muslim Brotherhood and would be more votes for him to count on later on. Why not? Rescuing them from the constant killing fields of Syria was a good idea. It didn't work, however on Vick. Vick may have been born into a Muslim family but was not Muslim in his heart. He was basically Jewish but had been educated in a private Catholic grammar school where he had insisted on attending instead of going to the Muslim public school. He had had enough of Muslim ideas in his little community and didn't like them at all. Usually, every discussion turned into a lesson with him being the teacher, using Socrates's method of questioning his debater. He soon became known as a defender of Jews and of Israel. It's a good thing he had turned out to be a boxing champion in college, as the guys in the neighborhood didn't dare take him on. They couldn't argue with his reasoning, either. He dealt in facts they couldn't dispute. Besides that, he carried the Golden Medal of Syrian Boxing Championship from 1999 to 2001. No one wanted to take the big guy on.

FOURTEEN

Now in Cairo, he dare not tell anyone that he was not a Muslim and that he wouldn't attend prayer services in the Mosque with them, not even once a day. In his heart he was Jewish, a descendant of King David, and he intended to learn more about his religion now that he was out of Syria. There was no way he could make contact with his computer on Jewish websites back home. All were forbidden there.

His neighbors in Faroh City were all rich Syrian refugees like himself but mostly all were religious Muslims who prayed five times a day. Rent here cost $800 per month. Water, garbage and electricity were included. The lawn was maintained.

Vick spent a lot of time in the coffee shop. He spent time smoking the hookah, a water pipe. It was entertaining for him to sit with men of Egypt who were so much more isolated than he had been in Syria and indulge in something growing less popular in Syria. There in Damascus, the religious considered smoking as "Makruh," something to be avoided, or God forbid, "Haram," meaning forbidden. He enjoyed the taste as a break away from smoking cigarettes, which he'd rather die than be deprived of. He thought he didn't have a chance of getting another job so didn't even bother to look for one. It was easier to just remain here, lost in the clouds of smoke with friends.

"Come with me," cajolled Yana's husband, Alaa. "Come with me to the mosque and we will pray together. I'll give you $1,000 if you come. Be a part of my organization and you'll receive $10,000. What's wrong with you, huh? Why won't you make your sister happy?"

"I won't Alaa. I'm not into praying. I'll do my own talking to God, thank you. I don't like to get down on my knees," replied Vick, who had devoutly refused all comers when they tried to coax him into Muslim teachings. He steadfastedly refused. They talked about it behind his back, and he was aware of this. But he also knew that he could handle himself since he was larger than life, taller and more clever than they were.

Vick then wrote to his Jewish American-Israeli friend, Deborah on facebook, and told her of his plight of being pressured to attend a mosque and how he was afraid of what would happen since he had to resist the tempting offers of money if he would just join his male members of the family. Even his sister, Yana, was part of the pressure. He asked for help.

She wrote back that on June 4th she had sent out a letter to "The Jewish Agency for Israel" to ask if there wasn't some way they could accept him through the "Law of Return," and that he was a Jew on his word only being he didn't know his mother's maiden name, which obviously would be a requirement. Especially for a Syrian, he needed legal proof of this. Sadly, he held no such proof. She had also sent out a letter to Rabbi Yossi Gerlitzky of Chabad in Tel

Aviv asking for help, hoping he might be able to track down a Mizrachi Jew named Liliane in Tel Aviv who no doubt would not attend his synagogue, but that was the only name she could find for a contact. She hadn't received an answer from either one yet.

His mind reeled back to finding many old books in his father's study. There were scrolls that looked very old, and ancient books that were dusty. One he found was all about the Free Masons. His father had died when he was only thirty-eight years old and Vick was only three years old at the time, so he didn't remember him. He had left his Masonic ring for Vick. Now Vick wore it on his right pinkie finger. Vick had studied English in school, and the book was very readable for him. He dared to post Masonic information sites on the web. The fighter in him dared to be caught. He never had as a smuggler or a hustler, and he didn't think he would be for looking at Masonic sites now.

One day in 2008 in Damascus the secret police had picked him up and took him to jail where he was kept without food or water for twenty-four hours. Then the beatings started. Being a boxer, he was used to taking punches, but had less of them in his boxing history compared to how many he had given to his opponents. He was young and strong and took punches that cut into his skin, grimacing with hatred for his assailants. His left eye was swollen and he couldn't see out of it as blood was streaming down his cheeks. As he glanced up, he saw a girl being raped and beaten and beyond her were several dead men, who had suffered more than they should have from the beatings they had taken. He underwent beatings and threats for three weeks before he was released.

"Oh God," he prayed. "Please, I hope my mother wasn't a victim here for being Jewish." He then realized what could happen to him if the police knew he had a Jewish mother. Here he had been living in Egypt for a year already.

Finally, after not being able to prove that he was a Mason, which he wasn't but wanted to be, he was sent home. After all, he was from the same neighborhood as President Assad, and had gone to school with his daughter.

A little digging on google while living in Cairo revealed that 3,228 Jews left Syria in 1973. Most of the remaining Jews left in the twenty-eight years following, helped to escape by Judith Feld Carr, though the emigration of these Jews was officially allowed in 1992.

"My mother must have been in this group," he thought. He knew that it was in 1994 that a Jew's home had been restored into the Talisman Hotel. How Judith Carr got people out was truly a miracle when their phone had been cut off and they were banned form traveling abroad and forbidden to talk to foreigners. Other Jewish homes had also been turned into hotels such as Beit al-Mamlouka, Beit Zaman and the Old Vine Hotel. Elite Syrian and Lebanese people such as Noura Jumblatt, Druse leader Walid Jamblatt's wife had bought these magnificent homes that were at least two hundred to three hundred years old. Some homes had been turned into boutique hotels, each with its own unique style and ambience. One night in such a hotel could cost a tourist $250 to $300. Now Harat al Yahoud was deserted and the homes had been neglected.

"Oh, which one had been his maternal grandparents' home," Vick thought, "and was it as spacious as his father's home of his childhood?" His step-maternal grandparents' home had a´huge atrium in the center with a fountain. It was one of the best memories of his childhood.

In late 1994, 1,262 Syrian Jews had been taken out of Syria. The young Rabbi, Abraham Hamra, was their spiritual leader who went with them. First they flew to New York where many had settled, and then later he went to Tel Aviv. Syria's government had allowed them to emigrate on exit visas on the condition that they didn't go straight to Israel. The USA had helped these Jews through the "Madrid Peace Conference."

"Why, oh why didn't I go into the Jewish Quarter and find the synagogue and ask about my mother when I heard about her in 2005," Vick cried out from his bedroom. "Surely there might have still been one person there that might have been able to tell me about her." He would have been fourteen years old when she had left Syria, and he had never seen nor heard from her at all. At that age he had just one clue that he had a Jewish mother or that Nola was truly not his real mother. What a pity! Why didn't she come to him to say good-bye? Why didn't she come at all and tell him she was his mother?

Vick did not know her family surname. "Was she still using his father's surname in a Jewish community," he mused? To make matters worse, he hadn't even thought at the time of trying to find her. Now it seemed like it was the most important goal of his life.

To grow up feeling unloved by his family was a terrible feeling. His stepmother then was always busy with his three older sisters, who were the children of his stepmother and father. Evidently they had been married and Vick's mother was a wife taken after Nola and his father had divorced. When he was ten months old, his father had returned to his first wife and presented her with his son and said, "If you accept him, I will come back to you." Of course, two years later he was dead from bone cancer. Vick was never able to know either his mother or his father.

He recalled the run-in he had had with his youngest step-sister, Emma. She had graduated in accounting and was taking care of Vick's finances from his own enterprise of the engineering firm he had started. Little did he know, but she took all his money and left the city. They couldn't find her. Like his uncles, she had robbed him blind also, and she was his half sister!

"Nola! I've got to turn her into the law! She's a thief," cried broken-hearted Vick.

"You can't!" screamed Nola. "She'd go to prison! Give her a chance, she'll come around. She'll pay you back!" sobbed Nola, bewailing how her youngest daughter could do such a thing. Emma was killed later on in a bombing raid in Syria. They never recovered the money.

FIFTEEN

"What is your last name, Amram?" questioned Deborah.

"Halabi. It means Aleppo," wrote back Vick.

Deborah started investigating and found out that the history of Jews in Syria started in Aleppo, which turned out to be a big Jewish center. Halabi was an Arabic surname, or "nisba," and denoted the origin of the person and that they were from Aleppo, or "Halab," of Syria.

"Good grief," wrote Deborah to Vick. "This might mean that your father had Jewish roots. Maybe he had also had ancestors who had been Jewish. Wow!"

This elated Vick to no end. He hadn't thought about this. His father was simply not religious, though Muslim from Muslim parents.

"Vick, Queen Noor of Jordan is Lisa el Halabi. Her father is Najaeeb Halaby, and he is Syrian. Lisa Elhalabi is the administrator of the "Federal Aviation Administration," CEO and Chairman of Pan Am! There are a lot of Halabis. It's almost like "Smith" in the states, it's so common."

"Wow!" answered an astonished Vick.

"It also means people who traded with Aleppo residents. Several different families took on this surname that aren't related to each other. Some have added "Al" to the beginning.

There are Jews, Muslims, Christians and Druze who use this surname."

"I think we were the Muslims, then," murmured Vick, thinking his chances of being Jewish on his father's side were too good to be true.

Deborah replied, "The Muslim Halabis had migrated to northern Jordan to cities like Amman. Others migrated to Saudi Arabia to places like Jeddah. Many Christians have migrated to the USA, England and other European countries. Druze are found in Lebanon, Canada, the USA, and a few other countries and Palestine! Didn't you say that your family had gone to Palestine before Israel was created in 1948? Your dad was born in 1945, a few years before. He even went there to bring some artifacts there, you said.

"I've heard that the history of Aleppo goes back to King David in 1010-970 BCE wrote Vick the next day. Aleppo meant a bigger land area than the present day city back then." Vick had no problem reading anything in English. Whatever he read, he'd remember with his photographic memory. Rarely did it fail him. It would astonish Deborah every time he would give her a lesson about something.

Deborah found out that the Aleppo Jews could have been from the 1492 Spanish Inquisition. These Jews were faced with conversion or moving away, so many went to Portugal. From Portugal they were moved again and that's when some went to Syria. Actually, it was the Visigoths in the 7th century that started persecuting Jews, and then the Muslims in 1066 when more than 1,500 Jewish families were killed in Granada on the Iberian Peninsula. Wouldn't it be fitting if Vick found out his ancestor was Joseph ibn Nagrela, a Jew who served the king of Granada? He was crucified at the gates of Granada. This man had been the builder of the Alhambra, the Moorish Palace in Granada, and he had based its architectural design on the Second Temple. Surely, he had the genes fitting for an engineer involved in building.

Vick shared with her that he found out that Jews who left Spain went to Islamic countrries that bordered the Mediterranean Sea like Italy, North Africa and Palestine. They also went to Syria, which was controlled by the Ottoman Empire and whose rulers welcomed Jews with open arms. Those who went to Portugal were later expelled from there. The Spanish Jews spoke Ladino, which was a mixture of Hebrew and Spanish, but nobody understood them in Aleppo, where the first Jews who had been there spoke Arabic and read Hebrew with an Arabic accent. Then along came some Italian Jews who were called the "Francos."

The Ottoman government didn't keep birth records for the Jewish communities, they found out. Individual rabbis kept records of brit milahs, marriages and deaths. Today, where would they be since all the Jews had left? Only Rabbi Hamra would know.

Persecution of Jews started in earnest after the birth of the state of Israel in 1948. Jews were no longer permitted to own property, travel or practice their occupations. They were persecuted if they tried to leave the country. That didn't give them many choices in life. The government thought that if they left they would certainly join the Israeli army and fight against Syrians in the next battle they thought for sure would come about.

During the 1980's, when Vick was a little boy, Jewish holy objects were being smuggled out of Syria through the efforts of Rabbi Hamra, and Vick's father could have been one of the chief smugglers, thought Vick. He himself had seen a Torah scroll in his father's study, he was sure. Smuggled out were nine ancient Bible manuscripts, known as the Ketarim. Each one was between seven-hundred and nine-hundred years old. There was a collection of forty Torah scrolls and thirty-two boxes where they had been held. They were first all taken to Turkey, and from there in stages to the "Library of the Jewish National and University Libraries," and also to the Hebrew University in Israel. They had to resort to smuggling because they couldn't get permission to take them out of Syria. "Maybe smuggling ran in the family," thought Vick. "Maybe he wasn't the first after all."

"Yes," she answered. "In 1948 there were at least 30,000 Jews in Syria. By the time Vick left Syria in 2011, the population of Syria was at least 22,505,000. Jews could not escape out of there on their own since 1948 at least. That's why they needed Judith Feld Carr. That was because Judith had brought their plight of being held to the attention of the world and raised awareness of their situation." Deborah was so proud of the lady she was trying to emulate.

"God bless Judith Carr," Vick said quietly.

"There was a Madrid Conference in 1991," Deborah went on to explain. "The USA pressured Syria and by Passover of 1992, they began granting exit visas to Jews on the condition that they not go to Israel. There were 4,000 Jews living in Damascus, Aleppo and Qamishli at that time, including your mother. They were called "Yehud Ash-Sham." A few families chose to emigrate to France and Turkey. A few remained in Damascus where their beautiful synagogue was. There was this final airlift by Israel that took place in 1994. They took these few to Tel Aviv, I think."

"How will I ever know where to look?" moaned Vick. He felt elated and let down at the same time.

"The New York group is made up of Jews from Aleppo and Damascus. Ha! The Aleppo Jews think of themselves as the smarter being they've been in Syria longer and Aleppo was the center of Jewish learning. They are praying in two different synagogues even though they live together in Brooklyn and socialize with each other," remarked Deborah. "Aleppo has the Al-Hayyat Mosque. It had been a synagogue from the 6th Century. In 1170 CE, Benjamin of Tudela found 1,500 Jews living in Aleppo. Before 1914 there were 14,000 Jews living there. The Jewish quarter had many ancient synagogues with the oldest being the Mustaribaha that was destroyed in riots in 1947, just before Israel was created and fighting the Arabs. This ancient synagogue dated back to the 4th century! Think of this, Vick. Your father could have Jewish ancestors. What are the odds?

"There were two kinds of Jews in Aleppo. There were the rich who were bankers or merchants and then there were the lower class Jews who were brokers, grocers, or peddlers," explained Vick from his computer where he had been reading up on their history.

"Vick, my grandfather was a peddler when he came to the states. He had been given a horse and a wagon by some organization which set him up in business that way in order to deliver boxes from the ships to the town stores. This is when his horse was frightened by a noise in 1912 and ran and he couldn't stop it, not being that familiar with handling horses, I figure. He was thrown from the wagon and hit his head and never woke up. I guess his lot was to be from the lower class, then. Lots of Ashkenazi Jews started that way in the states."

"Hmm," commented Vick. He was hoping that his ancestors would have been leaders of some sort. He continued reading out loud to Deborah. The lower class Jews were craftsmen, stall-keepers, cobblers, clerks, peddlers, porters or people with no skills at all. Everyone played gambling games such as Backgammon, which is my favorite game," Vick remarked gleefully. They also placed dice games and cards. We call Backgammon by its Arabic name of Sheshbesh."

"We played sheshbesh in Israel," remarked Deborah, "and called it that, too. Back to your mother," cajoled Deborah. "In Aleppo, women generally didn't work outside the home, but some became domestics for richer Jewish homes. If your mother's father dealt in diamonds, I'd say they were rich. Standards had to be pretty similar for Damascus as they were in Aleppo about who was rich and who was poor."

"My dad, too," chimed in Vick. They were pretty rich because my dad made all the money. He had a lot of brothers, though; too many!"

"Jews in Syria controlled the movement of their young girls. Marriages were arranged by the parents, so your mother was ahead of her time in choosing your father. Cousin marriages of all four kinds were practiced. Maybe she was supposed to marry someone else and broke tradition and ran away with your father. Maybe by 1979 most of the men in her community had left already and she had no one to choose from so fell for your father that way. He had been a friend and neighbor, and he was darn good looking," commented Deborah.

The next day Deborah explained to Vick about the Cohen gene that both Jews and even Muslims carried.

"Deborah, I'll test when I get to the USA or Israel. I hope I'm a J1c3d like the other Cohens," he replied. Maybe I have Jewish roots from my father. That would be nice. What a surprise that would be for my uncles," he thought gleefully. Oh how he wanted this to happen in the worst way! That would mean that he had Jewish ancestry from Aleppo for some 2,500 years since biblical times and around 1,066 years before the dawning of Islam. The legend told by both Jews and Muslims was that Abraham had lived in Aleppo during his wanderings after leaving Ur in today's Iraq. He was said to have milked cows there. Halab, the Arabic name for Aleppo, is the Aramaic, Hebrew and Arabic word for "milked."

"Deborah, do you know what my father's business was before he died?"

"What, Vick? You had told me that Nola's family was in the slaughterhouse business, and that was a connection to him, because he was a cattle buyer like my father."

"He was the first man to buy cattle from Denmark that was a dairy herd," he told her. Now he realized that his surname had something to do with his father's actions and business, accidently, maybe, but in life, were there coincidences like this? Wasn't everything part of God's plan?

"Yes, she replied, "and there was a terrible pogrom that attacked Aleppo Jews and about seventy-five people were slaughtered there and hundreds more were wounded. That was in December and ten synagogues were destroyed by fire. Five Jewish schools and one orphanage and over one hundred fifty homes were all destroyed as well. Ten thousand Jews had been living there at that time. People moved then to Europe but they had to start from scratch because they couldn't take their property, their bank accounts or any jewelery with them. Everything was confiscated. At that time the League of Nations or the United Nations wasn't helping Jews at all like they are with the Palestinian Arabs today."

"Now, what do you know about what happened to my Damascus Jewish ancestors," Vick asked of Deborah.

"Back in 1840, many Damascus Jews were charged with ritual murder and were tortured when an..."

"Excuse me," butted in Vick who had walked over the the frig and was looking in it, contemplating what he could fix himself for dinner later on. Sitting all this time with Skype gave him a sore back. "Is this the Damascus Affair? I've read about it already."

"Yes, it is. Let me just finish what I was going to say," Deborah hurried to say. "This Italian monk had disappeared with his servant. It caused a lot of European and Jewish politics to be discussed. This is a story of a murder and of the most extremes of human conduct and brings up the "Eastern question." It brings in a clash of local, international, religious, ethnic and political interests over a charge from the 12th Century in Europe."

"My gosh! I wonder what happened to those charged," inquired Vick, wondering if he had ancestors up for murder from these meek Jews. He had heard about this several years ago. Because of this story, he had laid low from any rebels snooping around his home in Syria as he wasn't about to kill anyone, even if they deserved it. He hoped they hadn't followed him here to Cairo. Deborah had written to Alain Farhi for information and he was just knowledgeable with those that had died for genealogy purposes, but she had found out that he had come from an influential family. Rafael Farhi, or Muallem, as an advisor to the Ottoman empire sultan. He was a Nassi, a President of the Jewish community and owned dozens of the homes in the Jewish quarter. His own home was the Beit Farhi, which was across the ally from the Talisman Hotel. Maybe that was his mother's surname. You never know, Vick thought. Alain was a businessman living in the USA but was a descendant of his. He had been born in Egypt where his family immigrated from Damascus at the beginning of the 20th Century. He is a true genealogist.

"I hope he is also into DNA studies," commented Deborah. "You both should get an autosomal test and see if you match up with any segments of your chromosomes. How exciting can that be?"

Vick is always bragging about the Syrian Arabic dialect being the very best of all the countries. One American Jew had to agree with him in 2010 before the Civil War broke out.

"Damascus has, in my opinion, the best Arabic dialect, and the country is incredibly inexpensive. There are good people to be found, and I am sure that if I told more of my friends that I am Jewish, there would not have been too much of a problem."

How little he knew. "Maybe as a tourist spending American money because they knew he'd be there for only a short visit, but just try to live there, my friend," thought Vick.

"Vick, said Deborah. When you repeat a Hebrew word, you sound just like the Israelis. I'm jealous. My accent isn't that good. I even love to hear you speak Arabic."

SIXTEEN

On August 2nd, Deborah had written to a lawyer friend of hers in her Israel Advocacy group and asked him about how to legally invite Vick to the USA. She wondered if there was some special visa or how to go about it. The embassies of Israel have been closed for longer than the American one, and she couldn't imagine how to get him out. Could he give her some information on it? Maybe, she qustioned him, that their Jewish community could sponsor him? She wanted so much to save his life, and felt it was in great peril. She reminded him that to save one life was to save the world.

At the same time, Deborah had been writing to an old time friend who had asked her to marry him. He was born a Muslim in India, but had a Jewish uncle that he loved. He was a scientist and really wasn't into religion anymore, he said. They started communicating and Deborah told him about her facebook friend being in dire peril. He couldn't understand why she was so gung ho about this one Jew when so many refugees were in need. She couldn't explain to him how he had captured her heart, though he was young enough to be her grandson. Besides being tall, dark and handsome, this Vick had a feverent desire to be a practicing Jew and accepted as one. That made him a different case from all the other refugees. She just wished her own family showed some of his zeal and love for Israel. He was her fairy tale book Prince Charming, and that was it. Like a geni in a bottle, he was too good to be true. How do you explain that to people? Here he was, wanting to be Jewish, followed every piece of news about Israel, and was at least a week ahead of her in knowing the circumstances of the news being he was right in the Middle East and her newspaper received it so much later than he. Besides that, he remembered ver batum as if he were reading a script, every detail about anything she mentioned. His memory was infalible.

By August 19th, Vick was trying everything he could to get a visa to anyplace. He had heard of a Schengen Visa. He could only get one to go to another Muslim country. It was possible to buy a visa through the Black Market, but that cost thousands of dollars he didn't have. He had a resume in his cell phone, but had somehow lost all his smuggling contacts listing from there. At least he was ready to find honest work as an engineer, or anything for that matter, if it paid well.

Laws about being a Syrian kept him out of Israel as he was actually considered an enemy. He thought of going there and declaring political asylum, but being an enemy stopped that idea as well as going as a tourist. Besides that, the American and Israeli Embassies were closed up due to rioting against them both earlier. You can't get a visa without going to an embassy to fill out papers for one. He was stymied for a few minutes. Then he thought that if he flew to Turkey and applied for a visa from there, he'd have to bribe someone he knew inside the embassy in order to get a visa to Sweden. Lots of Muslims were going there these days.

He thought he needed at least $5,000. Somehow he would bum the money from someone without being scammed himself. Being a young swindler as well, he knew the signs and would never let himself be swindled!

Harout, a friend in Syria, informed him via Skype that the Syrian intelligence was monitoring facebook.

"OMG," he thought to himself." He then wrote to Deborah.

"Deborah! I have lots of friends from Israel and a lot of posts that show that either I'm a Jew or support Israel! I wonder what will happen if they see that? Are they waiting for me right now? Maybe my name is flagged and when I arrive they will apprehend me on the border. Deborah! I'm very scared. This will be the sum of all my fears."

"Relax, Vick. Facebook should be secure. We're using Message, and that's private," she typed back.

"Maybe I have to deactivate my account before I go there, and I have to delete all my Hebrew books and all the pictures that express my love to Israel!" What do you think, Deborah?" It's very hard for one to hide his true feelings and his ideology and even his religion because he's afraid that it will take his life. I want to practice Judaism and I want to eat Kosher all the time and I want to speak Hebrew. Deborah, I love being Jew and I'm very proud of it thank God and I love Israel more than life itself, but what can I do?"

Deborah put out an e-mail to all the synagogues and Jewish groups in her large city asking for help for Vick and received one reply back from a good friend of hers, an address of a man to contact in Jerusalem and sent it to Vick. He collapsed on the daveno when he read it, knowing that he couldn't contact any person living in Israel from his residence in Egypt, or he'd surely be picked up again and held for keeps for being a spy.

Along with the cattle business, Vick thought there was something strange about all the artifacts he had found in his father's study. Deep in his mind he had a feeling that his father also dabbled in the antique dealings and had possibly even traveled into Israel and had sold some of these objects there, since so many were obviously carrying Hebrew inscriptions. His father, being a Mason, and a Master Mason at that, was one interesting character from a disgusting family. Who knows, maybe he had had a Jewish grandmother, too!

Oh, that his mother had been in his life, he wouldn't have been forced to hit the streets at age five selling newspapers in Damascus along with many other little urchins. It didn't take long for this tall child to find himself in the smuggling racket. He was bright enough to see that it paid off in more money than selling newspapers on the street corner did, and this way he could bring home money for food and gain some status in the family. Soon, he became the main provider besides being the only male in his family circle. For even though his stepmother was a dress designer, his money was often the only money coming into the household. Today, he realized he was one of the main smugglers from Syria who had a history of successes. He did have a strong conscience, though, and wouldn't smuggle anything out that would cause injury to anyone like any weapons. No, he dealt in money and jewels mostly. In Syria, it was good to have many talents. One of his that helped throughout his life was of having a photographic memory. Many a time that helped to save his life. All his life since he was a wee child, he had been the provider for his family, a family that had offered no love back to him.

At this point Vick looked around the apartment that he had grown used to with the garden outside that his cat loved to play in where he sat often with his coffee and talked with neighbors who were also Syrians, but more wealthy and secure ones.

He mused," Just less than one more month here and then what? Where will I go and what will I do? Deported back to Syria and then what? I will be dead in a second there! I'm willing to do anything to get out of this mess. Now what? Oh God, help me!"

Since 2005 when Vick had learned of having a Jewish mother, he had been busy working as an engineer and dating many women. Life for him was in that order; work, designing his American-style house, and sex. He thought of wanting to find his mother, but then felt angry for it was she who had deserted him.

"Surely, there must have been a good reason for her behavior," he thought. "Did they have an argument? Did his father steal him away from her? Whatever happened? Is it the truth, or was the stranger just full of hot air?"

He had dug around and found out that beginning on the Passover holiday of 1992, 4,000 remaining Jews of Damascus, the Yehud ash-sham, as well as the Jewish community in Aleppo and the Jews of Qamishli were permitted by Hafez al-Assad to leave Syria as long as they didn't go to Israel. Only a few remaining Jews in Syria were still in Damascus.

Several years later, amidst sex and debates about Israel and Jews being such nasty people, Vick thought about wanting to go to Israel to find his mother and get at the truth. Now, he played with the idea of leaving Egypt for Israel, but how! They were enemies. For a while, in 1981, Jews and Egyptians were at such peace due to Sadat that tourism was taking place. People could bus from Israel to Egypt and vice versa. This wasn't happening now. Both the American and Israeli Embassies were closed. Things had gone from good to bad politically. Morsi, the President of Egypt, was also a head of the Muslim Brotherhood's political arm whose charter was to destroy Israel and kill Jews.

Being thirty-three years old, Vick had come to the fork in the road of his life that he wanted to marry and thought that only a Jewish girl would do. He certainly didn't want to bring children into the world who would carry on Islamic beliefs, so he had to find a Jewish girl, and there were none in Egypt at all, only a few very old ladies. He put his creative mind to work to solve this immense problem. The only way a Syrian could travel on a Syrian passport was to another Muslim country. One had to have a lot of money to buy visas to Sweden or England, for instance. He was running out of money. He felt the same urgency that many women do when they realize that their biological clock is moving fast and it's time to bear children if there were to be any at all.

Being short on cash and alone, for his step-mother hadn't returned as yet, made life even more unbearable. In fact, she was now visiting with another daughter in Jordan, so Vick felt all alone. He was living below the minimum wage. This was a horrible come-down for a man who had had it all. He had one of the most extravegant homes in Damascus and a more than hefty income being an engineer and program assistant. He had had ten years of computer savvy in programming, photo shopping, MS Office and spoke English well, with Russian and Italian besides his beautiful native Syrian Arabic. He never again had been in need of money since he was a little kid until now. To even try to register as a refugee was below reproach. He couldn't do it even if it were possible. To face living in a refugee camp was more than he could bear. Life would not be worth living. He was a man of action, ideas, always on the go and always working on something. To stagnate in a camp? Never! Right now was almost unbearable as it was, to be so alone.

"Oh how the might have fallen," came to his mind. "Yes, it is hard and a desperate life." he thought. He realized he had no country anymore. He was stateless and unable to travel. "God," my Mercedes Benz 180 C is still in Lebanon with my best friend. Oh, how I miss racing along in my navy blue classy auto," He thought that once back in Lebanon, he would drive to his home in Syria if he was going to be expelled from Egypt. His friend would go with him.

What he didn't realize was that he was going through the same conditions that many Jews experienced that fled from Arabic countries after Israel was created. They had been required to sell, abandon, or smuggle their property out of the Muslim countries they were fleeing from. By 2002 Jews from Arab countries and their descendants constituted almost half of Israel's population. There had been a main exodus of Jews from Arab League states, and another mass-migration of Iranian Jews which peaked following the 1979

Islamic Revolution, when about 80% of Iranian Jews left their war-torn country for the USA or Israel.

"Here is the last Jew of Egypt," exclaimed Vick to his cat on his bed. "I need a Moses to lead me out to my promised land. What a Jew I am, a Jew that knows very little about Judaism and I am in Egypt where it all started, needing to get out also! I don't even consider myself alive at this point. If I die, who will claim my body? No one! No Jewish or Muslim person will say they know me because I'm alone, with no one now. Maybe I should take my life because this will bring an end to my suffering. If seems to me that I will be stuck here forever unless someone can help me!

It was this year of 2013 that Hezbollah entered the war to support the Syrian army. A terrorist organization from Lebanon, it was most likely that they would want to get an advantage in Syria. Syria was also getting military support from Russia and Iran, while Qatar and Saudi Arabia were sending weapons to the rebels along with the USA who entered the fray later on.

"Mama!" cried Yana to her mother, Nola over Skype in late August. "Urm Al Kubra, you know, that village near Aleppo, was hit with a bomb where Uncle Sami lives. The government's jet hit the school, too! Our cousin, oh Mama! I'm so afraid of what's happening!"

"Oh my God," whispered Nola. "What else?"

"It was terrible! A teacher reported finding his students and parents on fire! Everyone was screaming and he could smell flesh burning! He said he tried to put out the fire with prayer mats, and four people burned to death. The police who came in later couldn't tell if the dead were children or adults. They reported that the bomb probably was a Russian made ZAB incendiary type," sobbed Yana.

Nola commented that this was like dozens she had heard about that the government was dropping on the rebels this year. She remembered hearing that the Syrian Air Force was using incendiary weapons fifty-six times since November of last year. No telling where these bombs will drop, and of course they had to hit a school. Nola wondered if that was on purpose or an accident.

"I'm sure glad we live near Damascus," Yana wailed. "Maybe they won't attack so near Assad's home. Poor Aleppo people."

The death toll in Syria reached the news in Egypt and was over 100,000 by June 2013. Besides them, tens of thousands of protesters had been put in prison where widespread torture and terror happened in state prisons, of which Vick could attest to. Severe human rights violations were going on everyday. More than four million Syrians had been displaced. More than two million Syrians had fled the country to become refugees and millions more were left in poor living conditions with shortages of food and drinking water. In Muadamiyat al-sham, twelve thousand people were predicted to die of starvation by the winter of 2013 from a Syrian army enforced blockade.

Vick turned on the news. August 21, 2013 and the Syrian activists reported that the government forces struck Jobar, Zamalka, Ain Tirma and Hazzah in the Eastern Ghouta region with chemical weapons. It was called the Ghouta chemical attack. Anywhere from 281 to 1,729 people were reported to have been killed.

SEVENTEEN

September 2013

Just when Vick was due to board a plane to Syria, the airline received notice that they would not fly there. Chemicals used by Assad where causing people to die, and the UN was in an uproar. It was confirmed on the 16th that Sarin, a nerve gas was used, and used on a large scale. Sarin had been found in the environment that was tested and also found in the bodies of the dead.

Assad's government had resorted to chemical warfare on August 21st and September 21st of this year, just as Vick was attempting to fly back. What timing!

Though this was not new for Syria to do such a thing, the last time they knew of was in 1988 in Halabja. Now, eighteen rockets had struck Ein Tarma, which was only 3.7 miles east of Damascus and the Zamalka district right next to it. They hit very close to mosques. They also had hit Myadhamiya, which was 12 miles west of Zamalka. There, seven rockets had done the dastardly deed. 1,300 people had died horrible deaths from this exposure. Of course, Assad was blaming the rebels and was saying that he had not ordered such a thing. Who can you believe? The rebels were made up of several terrorist organizations, Al Qaeda and the Taliban. Then there's Assad, the master of torture himself. "A pity," thought Vick, "that he was also a doctor as well."

The death toll was now reported to have risen to 120,000 by September in Syria. Reports were coming out of widespread torture and terror in state prisons that Vick had experienced, and so he knew that this had to be true. The government and the rebels were accused of severe human rights violations. Amnesty International said that both in 2012 and 2013 the majority of abuses were done by the Syrian government. By now, more than four million Syrians had been displaced and more than two million Syrians had fled the country and had become refugees. Chemical weapons had been used on more than one occasion which triggered immediate international reactions but not action itself about stopping it.

By the 27th, the Executive Council of the OPCW adopted a time line to destroy Syria's chemical weapons. Then the UN Security Council unanimously voted to destroy Syria's chemical weapons arsenal. They plan to impose measures under Chapter VII of their charter if Syria didn't comply with the resolution.

Thoughts drifted back to living in his beautiful home outside of Damascus where he had so many parties. One day a girl had attended who was known to be a lesbian.

"I don't think homosexuals are living correctly," mused Vick to one of the attendees at his party. "I know I could cure Fatima. I know what women like."

"Sure," replied Elijiah. "A bet's on. How about a $50?"

"You've got it," answered Vick

"Fatima, come with me. I'm going to show you something that will make you very happy." Vick led the leery girl to his spacious bedroom and started rubbing her back, and then commenced to take off her shoes. He rubbed the soles of her feet. "Does this feel good?" he asked.

"Yes, it does," she replied, and she edged towards the door doing a two-step with Vick hanging onto her.

"You are going to lie down with me and see what you've been missing that your girl partners can't give you," he coaxed, and like a hypnotized person, she obeyed.

Vick hand manipulated her much as he imagined a female partner could do, and then he got on top of her starting making love to her. She reacted in kind. He stroked her all over and then commenced french kissing her. Gently he prodded and entered her, pushing a little harder until she grabbed his butt and pulled him down into her. Riding her back and forth, she suddenly let out a moan of immense pleasure and aggressively kissed him on the lips without any prodding from him. She had taken the initiative.

"Do you want a woman after this?"

"No, I see what you mean," she whispered, still holding him tight. "Are you always available for me?"

"No, but that room through this door always has those that are available. Just try them," he suggested. "I think you are cured. Good girl."

Vick read on facebook that there were about fifty middle-aged Jews still living in Damascus and they were celebrating the High Holidays that came in September. He wondered what that was all about and gave himself a mental thought to check it out. He knew his mother and others had left either in 1992 or 1994. These were people who were now from age forty-five to fifty. He thought a bit and realized that his mother could be the same age as thse people. Could she still be in Damascus all this time? He would plotz if that were true. There's a Jewish word he had just learned, plotz, similar to fainting or dying, being absolutely exasperated about something.

He read further and saw that Assad's forces were actually protecting these last remaining Jews! First he drove them all away by his cruelty and now he's protecting the remainder. He says he's not against Jews, just Israelis, but in 1992 and before he was against the Jews of Syria and had kept them locked up in a ghetto without any right. "Who's he kidding," he thought. Now he's up against the Sunni majority of Syria who are against Shi'ites and Alawites. Heck, the Alawites are just an offshoot of the Shi'ite Islam anyway, not much difference. The Christians, Druses and Kurds are playing it safe. They are neutral, like Switzerland. It's now amazing. He's witnessing the Jews siding with the Alawites who ae giving them protection. These older Jews are caring for their beautiful synagogue and the cemetery and that's all he knew about them now.

Vick kept up his own search of trying to find a way out of Egypt. He tried all sorts of websites that offered hope. Finally of the 17th, he found that Sodertajehas, a small town in Sweden, had accepted more refugees from Iraq than the USA and Canada put together. He started looking into a visa for Sweden, only to realize that the Black Market would be the only way, with a cost of about $5,000, maybe even as high as $10,000.

Then, Sweden offered a home to all Syrian refugees. It had a very open-armed immigration policy and had decided to offer permanent residency to all the Syrian refugees. If only he could get there. They already had 8,000 Muslims living in Sweden with temporary residency permits and it was thought that they would be joined by many more asylum seekers. The UN thought that over two million Syrians have left their homes looking for safety and prosperity. Sweden has realized that the Civil War was not going to stop soon, and that they are burdened with possible long term consequences. Sweden actually is in crisis mode over this decision because of the cultural and political differences of the two peoples. They have taken on this risk in the name of humanitarianism, though.

"They figure that the rest of the world will not copy their refugee policy." reported Deborah.

"Oh," thought Vick. Would this be the best alternative to Egypt for a Jew? I wonder if they have synagogues there," he pondered, "or lamb chops."

"Ah, hell," Vick cried out to no one in particular. "I've got to do something. I'm going to go diving." Vick had been on the swimming team in high school and learned to dive in Sharm el Sheikh and at al Aqaba, so he decided, since he counted among his talents the fact that he was a professional diver and licensed by the Blue Lagoon Club to bury his depression in diving. He'd do another 150 foot dive. So in the early part of September, Vick hooked up with some casual Italian friends from the diving club in a fishing boat and dove and fished all day and night in Taba, the city by the sea.

They went from Hurghada to Dahab by sea and on the way they met another boat full of people diving and fishing underwater. There were sharks swimming there also, but being true divers, they all respected all life underwater and that included sharks, so they weren't afraid of them. They turned out to be a boatload of Israelis on a pre-Passover vacation.

Vick, being very friendly and eager for company, did the most talking, and listening in the group was a beautiful tall female diver and when she took off her head gear, Vick saw she had long golden blonde hair. Her name was Galit. She was an Israeli Jew on vacation from modeling. Everyone in the group thought that it seemed as if they had known each other forever. He told them his whole new life story of finding out that he too was Jewish, and they said they would try to help him get into Israel. At night he borrowed one of the fellow's guitar and played and sang some favorite Syrian ballads for them that he had written. Galit spoke a little Arabic besides her Hebrew but not any English.

Before this meeting, Vick had another opportunity to meet an Israeli girl in 2003 in Sharm el Sheikh when he was on vacation and had told her about his finding out he had a Jewish mother, too. However, meeting this new gal was earthshaking for Vick, since he was so attracted to blondes and this gal was beautiful besides. He was suddenly smitten like he had never been before. He fair skin was now turning pink with sunburn. He made up a song just for her and sang,

"When your eyes open to dawn's first light, am I the one on your mind from the previous night?

You are.

When the hot shower water beads against your skin, am I standing there before you?

You are.

Then the workday is done, the ride going home long, is your radio playing our favorite song?

Mine is.

Your key in the door tossed aside with your case, I run to greet you, our warm bodies embrace,

The aroma of dinner I've made you with care, welcome, my love, In your heart, am I there?

You are.

Have I told you today that I love only you, in your mind as you search Wales' sky of deep blue?

Yes I have, Yes I will, Always."

They made love under the stars that night. Swearing love forever, Vick stroked her hair and smelled it, taking in the aroma of mixed salt water and conditioner that aroused him fully. Then his hand moved under her shirt which he found was braless and he caressed her bosoms and felt her nipples swell. She moved closer and touched his body with hers, pressing into him. He moved her a bit to caress her all over and she nuzzled up against him closer and put her arm around his neck, stroking it. Finally, off came his clothing and hers and they melted into each other. Then they surged against each other until they reached that final moment of satisfaction. They had to be quiet about it as people were within earshot. Vick held her close and kissed her lips and eyes and wanted to scream that he never wanted to let her go. She was the one. Finally, after thirty-three years, on this special day of September 26th, he wanted to be with this one woman for the rest of his life and have his Adam and Eve with her.

Several days later after she returned to Jerusalem, they were continuing their romance via Skype. Her family was against the romance. Being Ashkenazai, they didn't want her to be with a Syrian Jew, a Mizrachi. They didn't know the whole story as yet, just that he was Jewish. It turned out that her grandfather was a rabbi, and was more open to this romance than her parents were. She thought he could smooth things over. If he had been living in Israel it would have been another matter, but he did have an unusual story. If only they had known that Vick had no idea what his mother's maiden name was—this was the crux of his problem. He would have to be able to prove his Jewish heredity. Otherwise, anyone could come along and claim to be Jewish. There had to be proof. Vick did not realize the can of worms he would cause to be opened just yet. Wasn't it enough that they met, fell in love and wanted to marry each other? He was Jewish!

EIGHTEEN

Vick's first day of work at the coffee shop as manager started on September 26th. He was ready to fire the whole crew after that day for laziness and for not following directions. They were so much harder to work with than any of his building crew back in Damascus. He was called on the phone from his higher up boss and told to calm down and not threaten the help with firing and that a few had already called him about this. On September 28th, Deborah received a frantic message from Vick. He was heart-broken as his love life was fading away at a time when he was on top of the world and unbeatable. He would wait and wait for her Skype calls and it was killing him. When they talked, she was always cut off quickly and getting back to her job.

Deborah sent out a message to Alan Green on the hope that this man could offer some ideas as to how to Vick could get either into Israel or out of Egypt. She sent another letter on the same day to Alain Farhi of the Fleur d'Orient website, which was a genealogy site. He knew of the families that were buried from Damascus. Alain wrote right back telling her he didn't know or couldn't find anyone by the first name of Liliane, and just dealt with the deceased.

By the 30th of September, Deborah had received a few lines from the "Aliyah Department of the Jewish agency for Israel" telling her that they had forwarded her letter to the "Global Aliyah Center" in Jerusalem for their handling that she had written on September 26th. That was the fastest response she had received. It kept Vick buoyed up for days as that letter had been addressed to Natan Sharansky.

Vick was eager to move to Israel. He could taste it. He read everything he could now about this country of his fathers, he figured. A country that the world was down on needed a fighter like himself who could argue with the best of them as to why they were rightous people. Vick joined "Looking for a Job in Israel" on facebook and was able to converse with the possible 3,695 Israelis who also belonged to the site.

He stated his background as best he could when questioned by other Israelis, all of which were not native English speakers. Including Vick, they were all using English writing as their 2nd, 3rd or 4th language, and Vick was unable to make himself understood.

They started jumping on him in an accusatory way. He quickly notified Deborah and asked her to join the group and to bail him out somehow.

Being an English as a Foreign Language Instructor from a junior high in Israel, and English as a 2nd Language Instructor at the college level in the states, she giggled as she read everyone's comments and just shook her head. Nobody understood what Vick was trying to explain, and they did a piss-poor job of relating this to him themselves. "Oh, to gather this group up and teach them some English," she thought to herself. Deborah got in the program and wrote a dissertation, just about, explaining in very plain English what his situation was and who he was. Soon, people were apologizing to Vick, but the experience had given him a preview of what he was up against when he moved to Israel. Though Deborah accepted him as a Jew and even easily as a future Israeli, the rest of the country might not be so generous. He's going to be receiving a lot of resistance, and he was getting tired of it all.

The hell! He was getting nasty comments from Arabic facebook friends for his Jewish postings now, yet his Jewish "friends" were having a hard time thinking of him as being Jewish, all except a few. In a rush of protectiveness, he unfriended everyone except his three favorites. He even deleted the job hunting Israeli group from his list of friends. Enough! Vick had never been caught as a smuggler, and he wasn't about to be tripped up for being Jewish now. He would start covering up his scent.

NINETEEN

October 2013

On the 1st, a joint team of OPCW and UN officials landed in Syria to begin destruction of the country's chemical weapons stockpiles and building holding them. They actually began on the 6th. The Syrians were said to have to actually finished the destruction work themselves with the UN and OPCW team monitoring and verifying the work.

Hezbollah in Lebanon has 200,000 long-range rockets pointed at Israel that can hit any spot in the 8,000 square miles making up Israel. Lebanon's elite seem to be involved in only one thing; to kill Jews. They haven't looked into what their people need or want and there haven't been any improvements for them. They've forgotten what it's like to live in a free society. They're not really living, but are existing in a police state where the police are not in control anymore, but the terrorists are. The neighbor of Syria and Israel only has 4,196,453 people and have been overrun by these invading terrorists, none of which are Jewish. It was once a state with 60% Muslims and were ruled by the Christians, but now the Christians have been beaten down by a group of Sunni and Shi'a Muslims. Major Hadad of the Christians who guarded the border for Israel has passed away. Such friendship is no more.

A bright idea came to Deborah. She searched on ancestry.com for Halabi, hoping that Liliane actually had been married to Mohammad and not just shacked up with him, and found a Liliane Halabi living in Brooklyn, New York. All this time they had presumed she was in Tel Aviv. Deborah wrote a snail mail letter to her, hoping this wasn't a name like Jane Smith, so common that a million Liliane Halabis could be in existence. Anyway, this was THE city to find her Liliane other than Tel Aviv.

Deborah again sent out an e-mail to the "Global Aliyah Center" after not hearing from them anymore on October 4th and told them of how Vick had been more daring in explaining to people in Egypt how wrong they were to knock Israel, and how he had actually changed their minds. She told them of his being an engineer who could offer so much of his talents to Israel and how he wanted to fight in the IDF for them.

When his idol, Galit, realized he didn't know that this was a gigantic problem in which he didn't even know his mother's maiden name or that he hadn't been brought up as Jewish like other Mizrachi Jews, but as a Muslim, an enemy of the state of Israel, she shouted at him in their last skyping and said she never wanted to see him again. She felt he had tricked her! He was a Muslim and not a Jew! He was crushed. He would never be accepted in Israeli society, evidently, and the one woman that he fell head over heels for was screaming at him. His heart was broken. There was no point of going on. Death would be a relief.

By the middle of October of 2013, Vick decided to return to Syria and look for his records in the government offices about his family. He wanted to see his birth certificate. He had talked to his step-mother who told him that in reality, she was listed on the birth certificate as his mother, which she really wasn't. He had not been born in the hospital, but at home, so his father had delayed registering him by several days. He and Liliane were trying to decide where to do this, out of Syria or in, because if he was registerd in Syria, he could not have Yehud on the certificate. That was a death sentence. So actually he was born before the date on the certificate. The whole thing was a sham to get him through life.

At the same time he found out that his father's home had been flattened by rebels' bombs and there went all his hopes of his family records, including a picture of Liliane he had been told was in a wooden box in a drawer in his father's study. She was said to have hazel eyes and full lips. He had never known about the picture. All this time he could have seen what she looked like. One thing he knew, and that was that he resembled his father a great deal. When the stranger had entered his house, he said he thought he was looking at his father! He had been a terribly good looking man, and he had only one picture of him which he carried in his wallet.

"Deborah," Vick wrote. "I have a Lebanese friend who wants to get me to Ghana. What do you think?"

"Well, it's out of Egypt," wrote back Deborah.

"He's got a job and needs the English because the bosses are Americans there, and he doesn't understand well enough. That's where I come in," he replied. "He's got a

Ghana immigration service visa on arrival all filled out and I'm to leave on the 18th and it's made out for me to stay until November 17th. Maybe I can stay longer once I get there."

"This sounds terrific," replied Deborah.

Deborah did a google search and found out that Jews were in Ghana since 1976 thanks to an Aaron Ahomtre Toakyirafa who lived in Sefwi Sui in western Ghana. He had had a vision and spoke with spirits telling him that he and his friends were all descendant of the Lost Tribes of Israel.

There is a synagogue there and family living facilities in New Adiembra. Most of the community are the first generation of Ghanians to be Jewish.

"Vick." Deborah sent him a message. "I think you can teach them more about being Jewish than they can you. You'll all be learning together," laughed Deborah. Eight hundred of a core group were practicing Judaism. This community originated from Jews in North Africa crossing the Sahara Desert centuries ago, and ended up on the Ivory Coast. Some people had kept their Jewish customs, such as burying the dead immediately after death, and avoiding some meats considered to be unclean, like pork. They called David Ahenkorah a rabbi, but he thinks of himself just as a teacher, which is what rabbi means. He admitted that he hasn't been trained to be a rabbi. The group had a donated book about Judaism and told about Jewish traditions.

Vick called Deborah on Skype. "Listen to this. For many years, the Jews of Sewfi thought they were the last remaining Jews in the world. Then in the 1980s, one of the men traveled to the capital of Acera and asked the government if there were other Jews in the world. They then discovered, to their complete surprise, that there were millions of other Jews in the world. To be exact, there were about five million then in Israel and six million in the USA. The community traveled to the Ivory Coast and contacted Israel's government. Their embassy sent them one torah Scroll and a single siddur, a prayer book. Then in the 1990s a Michael Gershowitz from Des Moines, Iowa came from his synagogue of Tifereth Israel to learn about their history. He provided them with two hundred prayer books. The community named their synagogue "Tifereth Israel" in honor of the contribution.

Ghana is considered the first African country to establish diplomatic relations with Israel. In September 2011, they reopened its embassy in Ghana after thirty-eight years that it had been closed. Vick was looking forward to going there. He waited for his friend to call him back.

"Have you heard from him yet?" asked Deborah in a message.

"Evidently he couldn't scrape up the visa money," he said. The offer had fallen through, like so many other ideas that came his way.

His first job had fizzled out because of all the rioting going on in July in Cairo making it impossible to be out in the streets. So many businesses just came to a halt in Cairo and the surrounding areas. Finally, Vick had managed to get another job as manager of a large coffee shop, the same one he had smoked the hookah in. It only paid 800 pounds per month, and that money couldn't be paid to him until he had put in three months of work. He wondered if he would still be in Egypt by that time.

Vick put on his Cavalli shirt that was 100% Egyptian cotton, and blue jeans and looked the part of a manager. He strolled out of his apartment and found his car and chauffeur waiting for him to drive the 12 miles to the coffee shop early to be there by 7:00 am. There he dealt with flirtatious ladies on the prowl and a crew hired by his boss that didn't know what to do with their time. They were so lazy, they had to be told every step of their job. Vick was ready to fire the first one who didn't follow his instructions to bring the customer a menu when they sat down.

Vick finally settled down in the role of manager and went out of town to get a heater for the winter months which were coming up. The coffee shop held about one hundred customers and he had figured out a way to make more room and bring in more tables, which pleased the bosses, as he found out amounted to more than just one.

They invited him to an overnight meeting in which they wanted to meet him, and this happened when he was quite down at losing Galit. He sat at the table and didn't say anything, and they just stared at him, the bubbly young man so full of ideas a few weeks before. Finally, he told them that his heart had broken over a woman and they understood.

The next week found him dealing with two young lovebirds making out in the elevator, for this coffee shop was located in a large building and on the main floor. Evidently this was a favorite site to make love, in their building elevator. Vick sent the boy away and took the girl into his office. He talked to her and then called her parents. The father came in about an hour after the phone call. He was most grateful for the heads up about his daughter and intended to keep her on a tighter leash. Especially in Egypt, girls cannot be so permissive. Good work, Vick. Festival time came to Egypt and by October 18th, Vick was working harder than ever in the coffee shop putting in extra hours that meant he rarely went home during this period. People came and went and Vick was still dealing with problems such as running out of sugar that should have been delivered earlier. He found his grocery store near his own apartment had bags cheaper than what the shop had been paying, so he picked up several bags and delivered them himself when he came to work the next day.

October 27th came along and Vick was very very sick. He could not hold any food down and had the worst pains in his stomach. He had to stay home and finally get some sleep. His immune system was running down from overwork and lack of good food and sleep at regular hours. One is not a machine. This strong athlete was breaking down.

"Deborah," Vick wrote on October 30th. "Today I gave my manager my two weeks notice or he will have to work by the book. I cannot put in twenty-four hours and never get back home anymore. I'm tired.

"I have no one but u, Deborah," he wrote on facebook the next day, which was Halloween in the States. "Please help me."

Vick had been putting in eighteen hour shifts to make sure the help did things right. He wasn't sleeping much when he got home, either, so finally one day he fainted during the afternoon shift and was taken to the hospital in Cairo. His doctor turned out to be a lady from England doing her year's off hospital grounds duty in Egypt for a year, Dr. Barbara. Her co-doctor, Wilson, confirmed that he was okay, just needed some sleep and good food and was to stop worrying so much. They gave him some Prozac and told him to take one capsule every 12 hours. If he had a bad reaction from it, he was to stop. Vick slept for the first time in months.

Dr. Wilson and Dr. Barbara became good friends. He had told them his life story, not wanting them to think he was one of the Egyptians, and that he was Jewish. They were very impressed and picked him up several times late at night to go out on the town. Vick could show them the sites, and he drank along with them.

Vick came back later after being run over by some kids on a Honda that had bumped his leg. He began limping, and was bothered by it. Neither Wilson or Barbara would charge him any money, being he was a refugee. He had stopped taking the Prozac due to a negative reaction, but was doing better, except for the leg. Barbara had him go lie down in their rest area in the back of the hospital. She came in later to check on him.

They made quick love that afternoon, with Barbara directing the frantic irruption of immense feelings. She had had her eye on Vick from the day he walked into their examination room. She suddenly felt a release of tension that had been building up.

"So, do you feel better, now, my dear?" she inquired. "This is my prescription for your tenseness and lack of sleep. I bet you can sleep now, can't you?"

"Dear, so much better, thank you. This is the kind of medicine that suits me to a tee," he replied and smiled.

By the 27th of October, Syria had handed over their plans for total and verified destruction of its chemical weapons stockpile and production labs to OPCW. On the 31st, Halloween Day in the states, OPCW said that Syria had destroyed or rendered inoperable all of its declared facilities for mixing and producing chemical weapons. They inspected twenty-one of the twenty-three sites where they were housed. The two remaining ones couldn't be visited because of security concerns, but inspectors said that the equipment was moved out of the sites and destroyed.

TWENTY

November 2013

On November 4th, Deborah had a meeting with the shaliach at her Jewish Community Center. She had met a very interesting male shaliach long ago in 1980 before she had moved to Israel while in preparation for that great undertaking, so now she would ask this one how to get Vick to Israel. She was so excited about it that her hands were shaking as she arranged the stack of papers she had about Vick in a folder to go over with in talking with the shaliach. Surely she would know what to do despite all the problems she had been facing.

The shaliach was not on time. Every person was given the scrutiny of watchful eyes. Deborah didn't know this lady or what she looked like. To top it off, she had left her paper at home with her name on it. An hour passed by.

"Wow," Deborah said to the front counterman by the door. "Do you know what the shaliach looks like? Do you think she has come in already and I missed her? This is just like the time I waited for my appointment back in 1980, and that shaliach was almost two hours late. I came twelve miles to get here, and I was early. I wonder what's happened."

"No, I don't know her, but she should sign in here with me," he responded.

Finally a young woman walked in, glanced around and Deborah knew instinctively that she was the one. Yes, the woman walked over to her as Deborah stood up to greet her.

"I'm sorry, but I can't stay more than a half hour with you today," she said clearly without an accent as Deborah gaped at her with her eyes wide. "I didn't know that my boss was coming to see me at 11:00 am today, so I'm not free after all. Let's begin. Who do you want to help to get to Israel?"

Deborah spoke emphatically, telling her by starting with Vick's picture, which showed a most handsome man standing with a cigarette in his fingers and wearing sunglasses. That peaked the shaliach's interest right away, being she was probably a good five years or so younger than Vick's thirty-three years. After using up her thirty minutes, Deborah was relieved to hear her suggest they meet again tomorrow when she could give her two hours of her time. Of course she would come back!

The next day they went over all the points about Vick, and then the whopper was laid in Deborah's lap. Today in 2013, there are several types of shaliachs and this lady was not the type that helped send people to Israel, but she was a speaker in the high schools that informed students about Israel. Deborah almost wanted to keel over, but the the shaliach said that she would send this new folder that Deborah had compiled that weighed six ounces on her kitchen scale to her San Francisco office and hopefully they would know what to do. So Deborah handed over her new file she had spent hours making from all the letters she had written to the shaliach, and said, "Shalom."

That same night, Vick had taken Barbara and Dr. Wilson to The Nile, a very fancy restaurant in Cairo, and he drank too much, something he rarely did, but this was an occasion and he was happy. Afterwards, he was invited into Barbara's boudoir and they made passionate love again. She had plans for where they would visit this next week.

On November 15th, the OPCW Executive council approved the plan to eliminate Syria's stockpile of chemical weapons. They were going to transport the weapons outside of Syria and destroy the chemical agents in some country that they hadn't decided on as yet. They would start with the most critical chemicals by December 31, 2013 and the remainder by February 5, 2014. They will get them destroyed no later than June 30, 2014 and other priority chemicals destroyed by March 15, 2014. The Council was also able to verify that 60% of Syrians had declared that unfilled munitions for chemical weapons delivery had been destroyed. Syria was committed to destroy all its unfilled munitions by January 31, 2014.

Reports came in on Cairo's TV news that the Zaatari Refugee Camp in Jordan for Syrians had now reached 120,000 refugees. It was Jordan's fourth largest city now. They talked about it as being the worst exodus since the Rwandan Genocide and this was the third year of the Civil War already.

"Vick, it's a shame that nothing has changed," remarked Nora as they finished eating dinner.

"This is a disgrace on Muslims who can't come together to solve their problems with Assad. Saudi Arabia, Qatar,

UAE, Kuwait, any one of them could meet the needs of the Syrian refugees in Lebanon, Iraq and Jordan. They haven't done a thing about ending the killings going on in Syria," he retorted. "I wouldn't live in one of these camps. I'd rather die first."

"They say that six thousand Syrians are running from Syria every day. I'm glad we left when we did," answered Nola. "They're waiting until their neighborhoods have been bombed or someone in their family was killed before they have to actually escape out of there. I can't understand it at all. We had free doctors with Assad. We had free education. What's so bad about that?" mused Nola. Why did this damned Arab Spring have to upset our lives?"

"Nola, have you forgotten that in Syria, Muslims don't like Jews? Look at what happened to me! I lost my Jew mother!" piped up Vick. "I've heard things about how they had suffered under Assad and his father."

"So," said Nola. "Maybe they were Communists. Maybe they were as bad as your uncles say."

"Damn you, Nola!" yelled Vick, and he stalked out of the kitchen and into the garden with Fluffy, his cat. Then he decided to take a long walk in the moonlight to calm down, but what he really wanted was a glass of Jack Daniels at this moment.

Thoughts wandered back to Nola's parents' home where he had spent so much time when he was growing up: ten bedrooms and five bathrooms in a walled home with an atrium in the center of the garden with a fountain. He thought that was the best home he had ever been in. What he loved were the dinners that the family ate in the atrium. He had spent a lot of time playing in that garden, climbing on everything imaginable. One time he was almost bitten by a snake that turned out to be poisonous, one Nola's mother never bothered but left him alone in the corner of the yard. Nobody bothered to tell Vick it was there in the corner. He could have died from its bite.

Dr. Wilson called Vick. "Vick, Barbara was found this morning in her bedroom. She had had an asthma attack and died during the night, evidently. We're all pretty much in shock. She was a good doctor and great friend. I can't believe this has happened. We're shipping her body back to England tomorrow."

"Oh my God!" moaned Vick. "This is too horrible!" He sat down on his chair in his kitchen with a thud and held his head. "What now?" he asked Dr. Wilson.

"We'll have a memorial for her tomorrow. I'll come and pick you up so we'll go together," sighed Dr. Wilson.

"Another woman in my life leaves me," thought Vick. This loss was hard to take. He was beginning to think he was marked for life. First his mother, then Galit, and now Barbara. He had always been the one to love them and leave them. This hurt.

Deborah had written to the head of the Jewish Community Center on November 4th and titled it, "A Life to be Saved." She wrote in depth begging for help for this young thirty-three year old Jew trapped in Egypt because he was a Syrian. She asked him about getting an invitation that she had heard about in which the inviter takes on responsibility financially for the immigrant and wondered if the Jewish community could be up to such a thing to save one life.

Deborah received a frantic message from Vick begging her to find a way to get into the USA. He had been receiving some strange phone calls from someone who knew he was a Syrian refugee and wanted to meet him. He spoke good Arabic, so Vick figured he as a spy from Damascus, and he was getting very jumpy. Perhaps he had spoken to a more uneducated person about Jews, or maybe it was someone who overheard him speak to several men. Usually he thought he was speaking to a more educated group of people. He didn't like these last phone calls at all.

Deborah started calling immigration lawyers in Portland. Most of the time she called, and they were not available, or she had the wrong phone number as it had been changed, and she would work for a half hour tracing one lawyer. After getting tired of that, she finally investigated one resource provided by the last person and called the "Lutheran Community Services" number.

"Hello," answered an unenthused receptionist who sounded half dead with a very flat affect.

"Hello," stated Deborah emphatically. "I wish to speak to someone about immigration. I have a friend who wants to come to the USA."

Dead silence greeted her. She was transferred to another number and then it went dead.

"That did it," she announced to her computer. "I'm driving down there. I've got the address, and I can find this place easily. It's only about nine miles away."

Deborah got in her car, and after making only one wrong turn, found a parking place and entered a very large building.

"I need to see a counselor," she announced to the receptionist, obviously a new immigrant herself.

Within two minutes, a tall caucasian walked over to her and invited her into his office. He spoke softly with a Russian accent, for that was what he was, a Ukranian, new at becoming an American citizen.

After discussing Vick's case with Alexander for about forty-five minutes, the counselor caught on that she was merely a friend and not the mother of Vick. That shed a new light on the case.

Mrs, this comes under a different law. A friend cannot get anyone into America today," he reported. "A mother has a hard time getting her son into the states today," he said, and it's easier when the son is getting his mother into this country. We have so many that want to become Americans. This is impossible for you to do."

"But my great uncle got my uncle in by sponsoring him back in 1939," Deborah pleaded. "Surely there must be a way on some kind of visa."

"Sorry, he answered. "Obama had mentioned once that we would be taking in Syrian refugees, but it has not surfaced to reality as yet. You cannot sponsor your friend."

No wonder the whole Jewish community had not answered her frantic e-mail asking them to sponsor Vick of dubious Jewish heritage. Maybe they already knew and didn't bother to explain it to her. Maybe they didn't know and didn't want to be bothered!

"Vick," she told him when skyping. "I can't do it. A friend cannot sponsor a friend to come to the USA. There is no visa of any type for Syrians. Maybe you can come as a student!" she said eagerly after thinking for a minute or two when silence was her answer. Deborah had been very hesitant to offer herself as a sponsor for Vick as she was a retired teacher and didn't have the financial resources to do such a thing. Here she had finally accepted this responsibility and was turned down.

"Sure, and I want to come and study and convert to Judaism," he replied. "To come and study engineering would be wonderful. I'd love to go to MIT, but that would cost money. I don't have any money!" What I have was fine in Syria, but it wouldn't be enough in the USA. I'd need a higher degree. Besides, all my papers are destroyed in Syria. I'm nothing!!! I want to get married to a Jewish girl and have children. I'm getting nothing that I need or want.

For once, Deborah was tongue-tied and disappointed herself. All this time of trying to get him into Israel was coming to naught, and now she couldn't even get him into the states. The only place he could go was another Muslim country.

"Vick," she implored, "Alexander suggested Ghana. Lots of people are going there, and you could go from there to the USA eventually."

Suggesting Ghana to Vick was received like a man offered boiled beef liver when his mouth was watering for fried chicken. The idea fell flat when Vick spoke of the dangers and lack of prospects there for a job, and he needed work to exist. Nobody was handing out free meals.

TWENTY-ONE

Chanukah started very early this year with the first night starting on America's traditional day of Thanksgiving.

"Deborah, I have $4.00 left in my wallet, just enough to buy Fluffy some cat food and cigarettes. What can I do?"

"Once I was down and out and collected bottles to redeem. Does Egypt have this policy?"

"You want me to collect bottles? I don't have a car. I don't collect bottles!" he exploded sarcastically.

Okay, another time when I was newly married I was faced with this problem and decided to make cookies and sell them door to door. You could do that!"

"People don't do these things in Egypt."

My neighbor in Israel did. She took orders for cakes and baked them and then delivered them to her customers. You could do that," Deborah insisted. "How about selling your father's, ring, then. He would want you to do that to keep going, Vick," she suggested.

"Never. I'll never sell this ring," he emphasized.

"You could pawn it. Do they have pawn shops in Cairo" questioned Deborah.

"No, they don't have pawn shops. People don't do that. There's no way I can manage much longer. I won't have any Thanksgiving this year again," he said flatly.

"You have Thanksgiving?"

"Yeah, we always had Thanksgiving in Syria when America had it. We had turkey, stuffing, the works."

"Deborah, tell me why Judaism is important to you in as few words as possible," wrote Vick on November 17th. This was rather unlike him, as usually he was in the mood for talking, and this one liner seemed unusual.

Deborah answered after a few minutes of thought. "Because it is the basis for how I feel about people and our relation to the world. It sets down the Ten Commandments. It teaches me to not treat others in a way I wouldn't want to be treated which is called The Golden Rule. My admiration for its sanity, fairness, intelligence of its teachings makes me proud to be Jewish. That's why it's important to me," she wrote back.

Later, Deborah found out that this question was meant for someone else, another friend on facebook of Vick's. He probably had my message page up and this person's message page up at the same time and was going from one to the other. At least she had the opportunity to let Vick know a few of her thoughts.

"Deborah, I've got only $4.00 in my wallet. I have to buy Fluffy some cat food and my cigarettes. That's it. I can't go on this way. I need to work. There's nothing here for us refugees. It's not like Syria where I knew everybody. Only Fluffy loves me. I want a companion, somebody to live with forever. No one wants me."

Brittney came back into Vick's life on November 25th and drove over in her airport rented car to Vick's apartment for a ten day vacation. She had a great job in Dubai and had been working there since her graduaton in Lebanon. She entered at the right time in his life because he had run out of money and didn't know what to do.

Vick took her to see the pyramids, and she rode a camel. They thought of looking at the museum, but Vick was rather disappointed with it after being there shortly after arriving in Cairo with Nola, so he didn't take Brittney there. Instead, they went to the coffee shop and smoked a hookah, which was pretty novel for Brittney. Women usually didn't indulge.

They spent the time in her hotel, and on Thursday, the 28th, enjoyed a banquet of Thanksgiving food in the dining room. They had turkey, stuffing, mashed potatoes, gravy, the whole works that one would find in America, for this is an American holiday. Vick had been celebrating it all his life in Syria, a country or neighborhood who had adopted this time of giving thanks and enjoying turkey. Little did they realize that it originally stemmed from the Jewish holiday of Succot from the time of the Exodus. The Pilgrims that landed in Massachusetts were very much into biblical history and simply copied this giving thanks feast from the Old Testament that they also studied.

"Deborah," he elaborated later on Skype. "I went up to the table and had four helpings! I was given the funny look, you know, but figured that it was the time to enjoy!"

"You must have a bottomless stomach," laughed Deborah. She was glad he took advantage and stoked up on the food, for she knew this big guy could eat and eat and burn it all up. He was not a lethargic person, but always on the move; a doer, not a watcher.

"Hello, how are u," he wrote on a Sunday when he returned home. "Brittney left on Friday." He was back with Fluffy, who had been fed the whole ten days he had been away by his step-mother.

"Fine," she replied. "Didn't you think about asking Brittney to marry you? You seemed to have got along with her so well, an old flame and all."

"No, she and I don't like the same things," he wrote back. We both had time to spend together, that's all. She likes sex, and I like sex. That's all there is to it. She went back to Lebanon for an overnight stay and then she'll return to Dubai. It was nice."

Deborah picked up her mishpukah, Audrey, and they drove to Audrey's other daugher's home for a Vegan Thanksgiving meal. They both shared the same grandson, son of Deborah's son and Audrey's daughter. Deborah had been keeping her informed about Vick, her special facebook friend, that she was trying to help get out of Egypt and either into Israel or the USA or anywhere else that was better for him.

"Audrey, the wild thing is that Vick can go to a mall and see the same movies that we get here and at the same time!" Deborah was telling her in the car while they were driving. "Imagine how small the world has become. I had no idea that he could do that. Vick saw the same movies I have seen with Steve." Steve was Deborah's son.

"That is a big surprise, Deborah. Do you hear from him often?"

"Not all the time. When we do, it's not so much on message anymore, but we talk on Skype. Sometimes our conversations last for hours," she confided to her. "I try to write down some things to remember, but usually I get too involved in the conversation. Imagine, me talking to a handsome Syrian just like we are having a phone conversation. Usually Skype gets tired of us, though, and breaks down after a few hours. Ha! Darn, it is more interesting to talk to him than watching these stupid TV shows, though."

"We turn here, Deborah."

"One time we were talking, or was it messaging," recalled Deborah, and I had my TV set on as usual, and I guess Vick did too, or he was on his computer of course, but was also watching the same TV show I was, and it was happening at the same moment. We were both watching the same program on TV while we were Skyping. There's ten hours difference between us! I call that amazing. He's ten hours into my future and I'm ten hours back in his past. We are sharing the same things at the same moment in time."

"That's too much for me to contemplate," laughed Audrey.

"I've missed u soooooo much," Vick wrote to Deborah.

"I've missed you too, soooo much," Deborah returned. "Vick, I think your mother died. I can't find her anywhere. I've called a Brooklyn number and didn't find her there. I've written to a Liliane Halabi in Brooklyn and she never answered. I've studied the mind set of Syrian Jews and no woman would have left with Judith Carr without her child. She wouldn't have done that, Vick. Something happened to her when your father gave you to Nola when you were ten months old."

"What do you think happened?" he asked.

"I think she died then. Maybe she had something wrong with her and that's why she gave you to your father. She didn't have you in the hospital or they would have registered you then. Or maybe your parents fought and Mohammad came and just stole you away. I don't know. It's just that it was highly unlikely from what I've been able to find out that any Jewish mother would leave the country without her son."

Deborah thought to herself that maybe her parents had fought with her over the child and told her she couldn't come to their home with him. She had been living with Mohammad, after all. Maybe she felt remorse for leaving his wife and three girls and figured he could eat his cake and keep it at the same time. He got his son, finally, that Nola couldn't give him. Now he could have it all. Liliane was the loser. Disgraced in her family's eyes, she had nowhere to turn.

"What? Oh no! The refugees said that they only have rice to eat! Oh my God, and Vick hates rice. Yes, I'll tell him. Thanks, Julie."

"Who was that you were talking to?" inquired Vick, who just walked in the house from making a run to the store.

"Julie. She was telling me about the refugee camps," said Nola as she sat down with a cup of tea and a cookie.

"Listen, just ten miles away from the Syrian border is an unofficial refugee camp in Jordan where mostly people from Ghouta live. You know, that place where more than 1,500 people were gassed by sarin. This lady said that when she woke up in the morning, she looked outside and everyone in her neighborhood had died. Everyone was lying on the ground or in the street. She tried to bring water to them and put it on their faces but they wouldn't wake up. So she left the neighborhood and met up with some of the Free Syrian Army men who took her through the desert. She was afraid of meeting up with Hezbollah soldiers who would rape her or kill her baby.

"What happened to her?"

"It took her a few months, but they got her to a makeshift camp in Jordan where she lives in a tent with a little light bulb that hangs from a cord in the center of her tent. Her tent is a UN tent. In this tent are about twenty-five other people that sleep on sleeping mats. There are flies inside the tent. They think they'll all die this winter from the cold. Some of these people had just missed being in the chemical attack. They have few blankets or clothes for the winter, no heaters, no wood, nowhere to buy bread and no money to buy any with. Just rice. They have plenty of rice."

"Nice place, Nola. And you think I should go to such a place in January? Where are you going? To your rich daughter's home in Bahrain. So nice she won't accept me unless I go to the mosque with her husband. I won't do that."

"Well, this is what is in store for you, then, my dear. This camp I'm telling you about is not an official one. It's outside of Mafraq, Jordan and they wouldn't take in any Damascans, anyway, so don't worry. These poor people. They call this camp Rabeit na'eam. The UN doesn't recognize it, just the Jordan Relief Organization. They're having trouble getting donors for it. It was set up in April and the donors are from the Persian Gulf, and the camp is growing!"

"Nice," commented Vick, pouring himself some tea.

"Hmmm, you wouldn't think so when it rains. Then, the tent leaks and they have a flood on their hands. People want to have caravans."

"What's a caravan?"

"I don't know, some sort of structure that is small but you can stand up in it, and it sits off the ground so it stays dry inside. At this camp they have three hundred tents and twenty caravans that nobody can live in yet."

"It's not an official camp, though. Right?

"Right. They don't have water, food, kitchens, medical clinics, school or anything. Just tents. And rice."

"I know about the big camp in Jordan, Za'atari, which is about twenty minutes away from Syria in the east of Jordan. Eighty-thousand Syrians are living in there from Daraa." added Vick.

"Yes, they were talking about that camp. Julie said that everyone except about four thousand people were living in caravans there. They have public restrooms. In that other small camp the men and women had to dig a hole in the ground and use that. Ugh! In Za'atari they have schools, medical tents and even marketplaces. It's now the fourth largest city in Jordan! They live behind a fence and the caravans sit in rows in that desert.

"What's the downside to living in Za'atari, did she say?" asked Vick.

"Yes, lots of crime, and they can't leave or find work. Jordan has a ban on hiring Syrian refugees, but a few manage to work on a farm or hotel at night when inspectors aren't around."

"And what's happening in Ghouta now? Are there any people still living there?"

"Yes, Julie said that the Syrian army is surrounding Ghouta and they are keeping the civilians from leaving and keeping food from entering. They're trapped in there.

"Assad thinks they were helping the rebels," commented Vick. "Or maybe they were the rebels."

TWENTY-TWO

December 2013

Ramzan Kadyrov, ruler of Chechen, announced on December 4th the formation of a special unit to deal with the Syrian radicals. He was talking with Syrians who had made their way into the North Caucasus republic and those abroad. They planned on interfering in the Syrian conflict if authorized by the Russian president. They were the perfect people to go into Syria as they were also Sunni Muslims.

"Now Russia's getting involved," thought Vick. "Maybe my Russian can come in handy. If I go back to Syria somehow, I might get a job with them," he said to his friend Karim who was sitting on the sofa.

"Sure, and get killed for sure, Vick. They'll put you on the front line! I wouldn't go back!"

"Ah shit! Come on, Karim, we'll be late for the movies."

"Russia and Syria's government intelligence fear that Al Qaeda in Syria is plotting a spectacular attack on the Socchi winter Olympics in February, possibly using sarin. Al Qaeda in Syria bought the sarin nerve gas from soldiers who were supposed to be guarding it and now they are ready to use it. God, of course they would get ahold of sarin. You can get anything you want with the right amount of money, and I'm sure Al Qaeda could afford it. Those soldiers of ours must have made a bundle off that sale. What do they care!" remarked Vick to Karim as Karim was opening the door of his red Fiat.

"I don't think that when those one hundred fifty people died back in August 21st in eastern Damascus, that they were killed by Bashar Assad's army at all. I think Al Qaeda's Syrian group did it," Karim said offhandedly.

"Yeah, and Barack Obama and John Kerry know this and I think they deliberately have manipulated the intelligence in order to blame Assad," defended Vick. Both men still could not believe their President Assad could have turned on their own people like this even though Vick realized that he had treated the Jews there so terribly.

By Sunday the 8th, Vick informed Deborah that he could not go on anymore and was going to take his own life. He planned on using cyanide and would make it himself out of apple seeds. Deborah talked to him via Skype until 1:30 am without impressing upon him the need to remain alive. He was determined, a young man tired of the fight to stay alive in a strange country without a job or any future to look forward to. He was defeated and didn't care anymore. Besides that, the only thing in the house to eat was some coffee. No, his step-mother didn't have any money either, and he had only $4.00 in his wallet. This was it.

Deborah wondered what had happened to him to go from being normal after Brittney had gone back to her home and today, just a few days apart. "My gosh, did they have a fight, she wondered?

He would not consider living in a refugee camp in Jordan, where the Egyptians are planning on sending him and others starting the first of January, 2014 when their residence card runs out. Probably more than 120,000 Muslim Syrians are living there in squalid conditions, he had been thinking. At least 40% of all of the Syrians are suffering somewhere in the world, and one that is Jewish will become fish bait in a refugee camp, he thought. Each year since 2011 has caused more refugees. A year ago there were 100,000. In April there were 800,000. The UN just announced on TV that there will be 3.5 million Syrian refugees by the end of December. "I can't live in camps!"

"Oh Amram, why didn't it occur to me?" wrote Deborah since she could not get an answer on Skype by December 9th. She didn't call him Vick, but called him Amram, a Hebrew name that was the name of Moses's father and the name on his passport. Interestingly, Moses was considered a prophet in Islam. "You have such a cold-hearted family. Your step-mother, doesn't she realize after living with you what you are up to? How can she plan to live with her richest of daughters knowing you are financially in the red and leave you to your fate? I could not walk out on my son like that; it would be that we would stay together. Your step-sister in Syria with the children; doesn't she have a husband? Surely the fare to Syria is not that great that they couldn't sent it to you so you could join them, bad as it is in Syria. For if I had family I would want to be with them. You could be such a great comfort and help for them. Your presence would spell "protection" for them, real or not, you would be such a comfort. I can visualize you returning to Syria in lieu of winding up in Jordan's refugee camp before you take such a serious step as you have contemplated. My G-d, your mother should demand help from her rich daughter for you. You have been the rock, the savior of your family. Oh Amram!!!"

Lamenting this late message was his face book friend Deborah, who had remained faithful to the friendship throughout the last eight months. Amram had said on December the 8th that he was going to commit suicide that night. He was going to make a mixture of cyanide from apple seeds, and that he was hungry, had no food in the house, and was tired of struggling. He couldn't face going to Jordan as a refugee. He'd rather die, and so he had decided to end it all and was accepting the idea and happy about it. Here it was, December 10th, and she was hysterical, lamenting the genius of this man being wasted, zeroing in on his beautiful long fingers that had played the guitar by ear. Those fingers would be on a corpse still wearing his father's Masonic ring of authority that he refused to part with, not even in death.

Skype identification for Vick had changed in December to the five pointed star of the Church of Satan. She had to look up this particular star and found it on google to actually identify it. This came after she saw that Vick was on line and would click on it and up came Mohamad Mohammad who turned out to be a friend of Vick's. This happened four times, and so Vick thought that because he had used Mohamad's computer once when he was tutoring his son in English, Mohamad was now using his Skype name. Had he forgotten to turn it off? Being frightened that Mohamad was in actuality working as a spy for Assad, he had changed his icon. But to Satan? Good grief!

"All I can think of is that he was alarmed on face book when another so called friend questioned him as to why he kept on posting Jewish things, and scared him into posting a Masonic background on his wall from a Jewish one depicting the Jews in Rome being carted off with the items stolen from the Temple that is so famous," moaned Deborah to herself.

Judaism had turned him away from Israel and possibly, his birth mother. Islam was distasteful to him and he just couldn't buy into Christianity, though he often defended Islam and Christianity, he was definitely Jewish-minded to Deborah. Every time she would ask him a "what would you do" question, he would give her a very Jewish answer. She started to think of him as some kind of Zaddick.

So, being he had been so inured by us all, he got even with whoever he now thought was following him, the secret police of Syria or of Egypt, and erased everything and put up a Satanic sign. Good grief, did he know what it stood for? Perhaps not. On religion, he sometimes was a little naive. On politics, never.! No, she thought again. He knew what it meant and that's why he posted it. He wanted to scare off whoever was investigating him. They weren't going to find him talking on Skype as a Jewish person. It was his way of giving them the finger!

Finally Vick replied tersely that he didn't do it, and that he was mad at Deborah for telling her family about what he was planning to do to himself. She should have realized that he wouldn't. It was just Jack Daniels talking that night. Yes, he was depressed and at his wits end. But he was a fighter and always got himself out of Jackpots.

Deborah was overjoyed to see that he was still alive and had possibly read her many messages she had posted to him after his threat. It seems she had better arguments that she could think of in the form of writing than she did with on the spot thinking, and she hoped he would take one of them to heart. We are taught in the United States to take a threat of suicide very seriously and not to sluff it off. It's a stark cry for help. Deborah found it impossible to picture Vick doing it, but couldn't see a way out for him other than the refugee camp which he was resisting so hard. So, she actually believed he would do it and couldn't be consoled. This handsome man who had so much to offer to the world; she could not get him out of her mind. She thought that perhaps it was his way of getting her to do something, to take action in getting him to either Israel or the United States. Scare the heck out of her.

He was now angry with her, which was better than being totally despondent. He was taking out his anger on her. Who else did he have to blame? He had cut himself off from so many already. It was okay. Now, maybe he would get his thinking cap back on and make a sensible decision, for she admonished him quite a bit already about his pride being in the way of his life.

As far as Deborah could see, Vick had to make the decision of being sent to Jordan's refugee camp, Zaatari. She had told Vick that if she knew him, he would be the one running that camp, and far more efficiently than they were at present. He was such an organizer and a doer, and he saw things that most people did not that were possible. He was more Iike the ancient "Alexander the Great" to her. He could accomplish anything.

She knew that he was paid up for December in his rent, so surely would stay in the apartment. He had confessed that Brittney had given him around $1,000 to take care of that and pay his other bills to live in the apartment as well. It was galling to him to have to take money from her, the girlfriend he hadn't ever considered as wife material. He hadn't even considered that she would wind up being more successful than he, the little over-zealous Lebanese girl who wasn't quite as special as the Syrian girls. She was wasting her time studying business, he had thought. Here she was now, a leading employee of a fancy company out of Dubai, traveling all over the Middle East and living high off the hog, which she would eat occasionally! She, who would get mad so easily if he kept her waiting. He had sunk so low in her esteem that she had taken pity on him and had gifted him with money to keep him going for a month. He couldn't continue living like this, a month at a time, a day at a time, even. There came the point when all was hopeless.

The UZN team led by Ake Sellstrom that was investigating incidents of chemical weapons used in Syria issued its final report to the UN Secretary-General Ban Ki Moon on December 12, 2013. The report found that chemical weapons were likely used in five of the seven attacks that they had investigated. The nerve agent of sarin was most likely used in four out of the seven attacks. One was the large scale attack on a Damascus suburb in August.

Friday the 13th, and a snowstorm hit the Middle East. Jerusalem was covered with snow which brought traffic to a standstill. Though a beautiful sight, it's occupants weren't prepared to work under such conditions.

In Amman, Jordan, 120,000 Syrian refugees woke up to see snow had hit their tent city. They were one of the few Arabs who were used to snow in the wintertime, and at home had been prepared and enjoyed it. Living under tents was a new experience for these modern-day Arabs, however, and they scrambled to batten down their tents against torrential rains and high winds on their second day of experiencing a very blustery storm that they called Alexa.

Lebanon was of course hit as well as northern Syria which was also in the path of this storm. The temperature fell all over the region to below zero and brought rain and snow. In Israel and Judea-Samaria, government offices and schools hunkered down and shuttered their windows. Deborah had taught English in Safed, Israel in a junior high which had no central heating. She used to teach in her coat all day because of it during the winter. Safed was at the same elevation as Jerusalem, so they were often hit with snow, but she had never experienced this cold a weather.

In Za'aari refugee camp, the wind toppled ten tents during the night of the 12th. The occupants of those tents were left to face freezing temperatures. One thirty-six year old resident reported that it was also muddy and he just wanted to protect his wife and four children. Aid workers came to him quickly and evacuated the family and others who also had tents that had blown down to other more secure places in the camp. Wadah Hmoud said that after having two days of heavy rain, the camp had been flooded in many places. Aid workers were trying to replace tents with housing units for the whole camp.

Jordan was suffering from power disruptions. Roads were blockaded and motorists were stranded, just like in places around Jerusalem and Safed. The snowstorm was thought to continue throughout Friday the 13th and onto Saturday.

Kids everywhere threw snowballs and built snowmen. There was some good out of it, after all. By mid afternoon, though, the snow had turned to cold rain and streets became slushy. In the Gaza Strip, the Health Ministry reported that authorities had to evacuate thirty people and take them to hospitals. They had to move others into shelters because the heavy rains also caused flooding and power outages there as well. These Middle Eastern Arabs were not used to dealing with this kind of problem.

Vick watched the TV news and thought how he would have enjoyed the snow. He would have been able to size up the camp and have tents tied down to face the storm if he had access to the weather forecasting. He hated Egypt because their weather was always hot. They never experienced different seasons. The only thing different for him, this second year of living here, was that winter had become tolerable to a liveable 65 degrees Fahrenheit and he enjoyed taking walks about Faroh City now. At least he would enjoy it if he felt a little stronger, for going without food was making him feel weak and a little cross. He kept thinking that a glass of Jack Daniels would be so nice!

What would he do when New Years rolled around? There would be no celebrating a New Year. The New Year looked as bleak as expecting the end of the world to him.

Deborah hadn't given up searching for help for Vick. She ran into this website on Thursday, the 12th.

TWENTY-THREE

2015 Diversity Visa Lottery Registration Begins

The U.S. embassy announces that applications for the 2015 diversity Visa (DV) Lottery will be accepted online beginning noon Eastern Daylight Time (EDT) on October 1, 2013, and ending at noon eastern Daylight Time (EDT) on November 2, 2013. This annual program makes U.S. immigrant visas available through a computer-generated random lottery drawing to persons who meet the eligibility requirements.

The Department of State will only accept completed Electronic Diversity Visa (E-DV) Entry Forms submitted electronically at www.dvlottery.state.gov during the registration period. Paper entries will no longer be accepted. No fee is charged for entry in the annual DV program."

Senator Wyden's secretary never mentioned this, but Deborah saw it didn't help Vick. It ended already on the 2nd of November. It was open for one month only. Vick would have had to scrounge for over a year and then it was like winning the Reader's Digest Sweepstakes. One never does.

This reminded her of when Vick had filled out another application to win a trip to Los Angeles for the Oscars. He was dreaming of winning and wearing a tux that the Actor's Guild would provide for him. That was a wonderful wishful experience for this guy who had done a little acting in college. How that would have been a great way to enter the USA. She didn't dare laugh when he told her so excitedly about the opportunity. Fat chance, she thought, but then Vick had been so lucky in so many things before. Maybe he would win it when they saw his picture. Heck, he could even get a screen test out of the deal and then he'd be able to stay for sure, for he had the most engaging, the sexiest voice, the greatest accent she had ever heard.

"Darn! Obama was going to bring in Syrian refugees. He hasn't allowed any in at all.

There's no way I can help Vick," complained Deborah to her cousin.

"We can't afford anything when we're borrowing money from the Chinese to pay our bill. We've got people unemployed here!" her cousin replied. "Aid for 17,800 people in Oregon is going to be cut off in three weeks. We have more than one million nationwide on unemployment that will see all their benefits end on the 1st of January."

"That's when Vick feels he'll be emigrating to some refugee camp," Deborah exclaimed. "The first of January holds a lot of fear for everyone. No Happy New Year ringing in this year."

"Vick, come quick! Look outside!"
"What is it, Nola? I thought you were packing."

"Look! Snow! Here in Egypt!" Just like back home in Damascus!"

"Oh my God! It's so beautiful!" Vick ran out in his bare feet and scooped up the snow. "I love snow!" he shouted. "It's a sign, Nola, it's a sign. Things are going to get better for me!"

"Maybe so, Vick. You always did love the snow and you've been complaining for so long about the constant heat here. Let's turn on the TV and see what they say about it. I thought it never got even cool in Egyipt."

The weatherman came on after about five minutes of reporting about robberies happening in Cairo. "The last recorded snowfall in Cairo was more than one hundred years ago, ladies and gentlemen." The next picture showed children of the suburbs playing in the white covered streets and adults looking up at the sky and tweeting pictures of the snow-dusted parks and squares. Then the camera zoomed in on the domes of mosques and minarets that were covered with snow. The news then centered on other snow-covered areas in the Middle East. They saw Syrian refugees in Jordanian and Lebanese camps suffering in the cold that covered their tents; pictures of Israel's army digging out stranded motorists as three feet of snow had hit Jerusalem which closed their roads making thousands in and around the city without power. They showed Israeli soldiers and police rescuing hundreds trapped in their cars from the snow and ice. Then the camera picked up the West Bank where the olive trees were bending under the weight of the snow.

"Judea and Samaria," corrected Vick to the announcer over the words, "West Bank."

Nola gave him a scowl. "Vick, why do you say that?"

"Because it's not the real name, Nola. "That's Judea and Samaria!" he said defiantly. "It was Jordan who renamed these places after they took them over in 1948 when they were already designated by the League of Nations to be a part of the Jewish Homeland!"

"You drive me crazy, Vick. It's embarrassing for me when you keep speaking out defending these people!"

"Tough shit, Nola. They're my people!"

"Really? Then why won't they let you in Israel?"

Vick now gave her a big scowl and ignored her comment. "They're much higher up than we are," Vick answered. "Jerusalem is set in high hills. So is Safed. They probably have a lot of snow, too. That's the home of Kabbalah. Mt. Hermon is nearby and they ski there most every year. I bet they'll do a rip-roaring business this year!"

"Here we are in Cairo enjoying snow," sighed Nola. "Over one hundred years they haven't had snow and the year we come in a hurry, forgetting all our warm clothing, it had to snow!"

"Yeah, I know," Vick said, shaking his head and reaching for a cigarette from his last pack. "I'm glad my shoes don't have any holes in the soles. They're Italian. I brought one sweater with me that's already three years old. It'll have to do. Flip the switch and see if there's anything about Syrian refugees," ordered Vick.

"Nothing has been happening. No one wants us," said Nola, her voice cracking. "Here, listen."

"Only five countries in the Middle East have participated in taking in refugees from Syria," the commentator just announced. "Europe has failed in helping out by only accepting a small number of people escaping the terrible Civil War. in Syria. They have maltreated people who have tried to get into their country. This was reported by Amnesty International on Friday the 13th. Even the USA who says to send them their tired and needy is not accepting any Syrians. Out of the 2.3 million Syrians needing a haven, it is only the five countries of the Middle East who have already taken in 97% of them of which half are children. The European Union has pledged to take in only 12,340. That, ladies and gentlemen, is only less than 1%. That remains a pledge, not an action. The one country doing the most is Sweden! They are taking in an unlimited amount of Syrian refugees. The only problem with them is that the Syrians need a visa to get there, and a Syrian cannot get a visa outside of any Middle Eastern country. How are they to get there?" asked the commentator.

"I know," signed Vick. "I've looked into it. I'd love to go to Sweden, but on a Syrian passport? Forget it! Nobody wants us. We're doomed!"

Vick woke up late in the day after spending a sleepless night. Nola and three of her neighbor lady friends were in the kitchen, talking. "Listen, Deena, I just got a phone call from my daughter's friend in Lebanon and ten Syrian children in the refugee camp there died after two days from the cold. You know the refugee camp there is out in the open. They're living in makeshift shacks and tents."

"Deena piped up, "No food or any type of aid can be delivered to any Syrians, either! They're as bad off as the refugees outside of Syria in camps. Assad doesen't let anything go into the territories he thinks are anti-regime."

"Even bread bakeries are closed," added Amira. Homes have been destroyed. What can we do for them? Nothing! Thank Allah we came here in time. What are you going to do, Nola?

"Give you some more tea," she answered.

"I know, Deena sputtered. We can send letters to the Russian Embassy so that maybe the Russian army can deliver some aid boxes there. Ladies, let's make up some aid boxes!"

"First, let's see if the Russians are willing," thought Nola aloud. "I think there are those of us right here in Faroh City who also need some aid boxes," she thought to herself, and reported to the group after thinking about it for a minute. Should she let them know that they are not well off?

"Maybe things will change and we can move back to Damascus," Vick commented rather hopefully to his neighbor lady, Aya, also a Damascan Syrian who was an heiress to her late husband's fortune. She and Vick were having tea with Vick and Nola in Vick's apartment.

They had been watching the news on TV that had been discussing the Danish and Norwegian ships that would be ferrying tons of the dangerous chemical weapons out of Syria.

"What kind of containers would those chemical compounds be in?" asked Nola.

"I don't know, but somehow they mix them together and they make Sarin and VX gases, whatever that is," answered Aya.

"Did you hear that they'll keep those containers at opposite ends of the two cargo ships?"

"Wow, I'd hate to be a part of that crew," said Nola.

"Hmm. They have no idea just how much they'll be taking out of Syria, but they can ferry up to 500 tons, they think," added Vick.

"They plan on taking these containers to some harbor. They won't say what country. Who would offer to take them, do you think?" questioned Nola.

"Maybe Italy?" suggested Aya.

"The ship will neutralize the chemicals first. How are they ever going to do that when they're in containers? They'll do that at sea and some of the containers will have to get more treatment than others. How will they know which boxes or cans?" pondered Vick.

"Sounds crazy to me, "said Aya as she poured herself some more tea and took a few cookies off the plate.

"Maybe they have to take these containers somewhere else to get more treatment. How are they going to do that?" asked Nola.

"What if the weather is bad? Even the sea can get might rough, just like the oceans. It's December and this happens now," commented Aya.

"I think that the safest thing to do is to sail into the harbor and do it there," added Vick. "They're putting all the sea life in peril anyway, no matter where they do it." Ah, now I remember. It was Croatia who said they'd consider letting one of their ports be used for this, for the transfer of the containers as long as no Croatians oppose the idea. Of course he must think that they'll be paid well if they do this, and it should show their cooperation with the EU. No one does anything without getting something out of it," philosophized Vick.

"No, I don't think these cargo ships will take any chemical weapon containers onto their ship until a harbor is decided on for sure. From there they will go onto an American ship. I just heard that on the news when you all were talking," reported Nola.

"Well, the important thing is to get all those chemicals out of Syria and out of the hands of the rebels, said Aya. No one wants to go back and get gassed. It stands to reason that once they were in the hands of the soldiers, it wouldn't take long before the Taliban or Al-Qaeda would get them. They don't care if they get gassed by gassing all of us; they'll all go to their seventy-two virgins," said Aya bitterly. "Then all we have to worry about are the helicopters and jets flying around bombing. But I don't think that can happen over Damascus. Most of us are pretty much for Assad."

"We'd better be," laughed Nola. He lives right nearby. We haven't suffered with him. Only Vick has, because his mother was....never mind. Have some more cookies?"

"Do you think we will ever be able to go home?" asked Nola. "I miss my work. Designing clothes gave me such pleasure that I don't feel anymore, no matter what I'm doing these days."

"Think of me, Nola," answered. Vick. Even sex isn't pleasurable like it used to be."

"Oh, you," she said, shaking her head in embarrasment.

"Look what's happening in Aleppo," said Vick as he was reading the morning newspaper he had picked up at the store when he went to buy cigarettes and tomatoes. "Talk between the Syrian opposition and Assad's government are to begin on January 23rd in Montreux, Switzerland in a hotel there. Wouldn't I love to be a little bird listening in on that talk!" he said dramatically.

"Hmmm. Because of that, the government is doing their best to kill off the people of Aleppo first before the meeting takes place. They've killed over one hundred in the past three days already there. Aleppo is where most of the rebels have dug in," Nola answered.

"Yeah, Secretary General Bana Kii-moon has demanded a cease-fire. Good lord, over 120,000 have been killed already. It's been almost three years of fighting."

"Who would have guessed," replied Nola. "That's where I did a lot of business. It's the center of business deals, the commercial hub of Syria. The rebels have held it now for more than a year."

"It's the Syrian National Council who is angry with the world because they have failed to take a real position to stop Assad. In the Shaar district alone, airstrikes killed fifteen people, and that includes two children from bombing from the air."

"Ha, ha! Russia and the United States will be brokering the talks," continued Vick. How can they even agree with each other let alone get Syrians to take their lead." What do you think, Nola? What will happen? Will Syria stop and sign a peace contract with these rebels? Which ones will be peaceful? Hezbollah? Al Qaeda? Ha!"

"Neither one, Vick."

"Once upon a time, Aleppo was the town of the Jews. They called it Aram-Zobah. It dates back so far that it's one of the oldest cities in the world," Vick said thoughtfully as he remembered visually something he had read about Aleppo on the internet. "Back in the 1100s, 1,500 Jews lived there. Imagine! No Jews live in Syria today! Then in 1492 from the Spanish Inquisition, many Jews of higher learning came fleeing death and the city became even more alive. Just before the First World War there were 14,000 Jews living in Aleppo! Maybe my father's ancestors were one of them.

"Nonsense, Vick. Your father was a Muslim!" frowned Nola.

"Yes, I know, but the family could have been Jewish originally, or Samaritan, or even Christian. I'm going way back, and the majority not too long ago were Jews!" he asserted. In fact, we could have even been Kurds, but I doubt that the most,

"Why Kurds?"

"There was a Suleiman al-Halabi who was born in 1777 in the village of Kukan between Aleppo and Afrin. His father was religious, named Mohammad Amin, who worked selling butter and olive oil. When Suleiman was twenty years old, his father sent him to Cairo, Egypt to study Islamic sciences at Al-Azhar Universtiy and after three years he returned to Kukan where he learned that his father had lost a lot of his money and was very poor which caused him to be fined heavily and the government taxed him. He couldn't pay anybody off so they put him in prison. When Suleiman tried to get his father ouf of prison, the authorities offered him a deal. He was to assassinate the French Army General, Jean Baptiste Kleber in Cairo, so he agreed. He got back to Cairo, dressed himself as a beggar on June 14, 1800 when he was 24 years old now, and did it. He had stabbed him four times with a stiletto. He was found, arrested and tortured. His right arm was burnt to the bone while he denied any knowledge with a Sheikh or any of the popular resistance movements, and then was sentenced to death by impalement. So anyway, Alhalabi could be Kurdish, too."

"Today the Kurds of Syria have the Democratic Union Party in Syria. You know, the PYD. It's been the main target of arrests and pressures since they founded this party. Members have been tortured and arrested. In 2004 the activist, Nazleh Kjel who was in a woman's organization. Turkey and Syria are always fighting against the Kurds. They have some security agreements between them. Syria has signed manay international agreements against torture but. we know what happened to me. I was tortured."

"Well, then. What happened to all of the Jews in Syria?" asked Nola innocently.

"When the UN decided to partition Palestine in November of 1947, the Muslims rioted against creating a Jewish state. So the Syrian Jews, who were being attacked, left the country. They went to the United States or to the new state of Israel." Vick paused and then asked, "How many Jews were in Aleppo when Liliane was still here, do you think?"

"I don't have the faintest idea," Nola said.

"They had about four hundred. Only four hundred out of thousands from Aleppo. There weren't many left in Damascus, either, where her family was from! I wish I had gone into the Yahud neighborhood and explored it. Heck. The riots destroyed one of their oldest synagogues, the Mustaribah. It dated back to the 10th Century! A famous scroll from then did make it to Israel, though that dated back to the 4th Century. It could even be that my father had found it and took it to Israel, Nola. I think he did things like that," said Vick proudly.

"He might have. He was gone on trips all the time," said Nola softly, reminiscing. "Here he may have saved the Jews special documents but the Jews of today won't lift a finger to save you, huh!"

"You keep rubbing it in. Shut up about it, will you!. Sorry, you're right. They won't even answer any of the letters Deborah has sent asking them to let me in," a sullen Vick replied.

"I remember your father talking about finding a cave when he was just seven years old on a picnic with his family near Damascus. In there he found a jar with something special in it that he took out."

"That probably was his start of looking for ancient manuscripts and objects," Vick replied. Just like I got started in my line of work. Ha! Nola, when we get out of this, I want to have my DNA tested. Deborah told me all about it. I can test my male side and find out who I match up with; Jews, Samaritans, Kurds. It will go all the way back in history."

"Who do you think you came from?" She asked quizzically.

"I hope the Jews. I hope my father came from them. I hope I have the Cohen gene, J1. If not, there might be genes from the Phoenicians that go back to the bible days, too. Then long ago the Assyrians overran the land. There might even be some Greek genes I'm carrying. No doubt I have Arab genes, too, because the Arabs came along in about 634 CE to Syria. Damascus has always had less Jews than Aleppo, but in the 12th Century, this Benjamin Tudela, a writer, said that there were 3,000 Jews in Damascus. And 2,000 Jews in Palmyra, and then of course many came to our city after the 1492 persecutions in Spain. Maybe that's where I cam from on my mother's side. I could have Jew genes from both my parents!"

"Shhh, don't say that out loud. You know Jews are the worst around here. Nobody likes Jews after what they did in the 1967 War," whispered Nola while looking at the door, afraid somebody might walk right in on their converstion about Jews.

"I know, Nola. We attacked Israel and lost. We attacked in 1948, too, and lost. We've lost every war against Israel. That's how Israel got the Golan Heights. We shot at them too many times from there and hit too many of their homes. Good! I'm glad that Israel won.!"

"Oh Allah! He doesn't know what he's saying," frowned Nola as she threw a magazine at him. "Still happy now even though Israel is ignoring you? Maybe they even think you're a terrorist trying to get in!"

"It's because of our leaders' craziness against Jews that led us into all these wars against Israel in the first place, Nola. Ever since the Jews came back and created Israel, Syria has kept to its old myths about Jews drinking blood and such and have kept up this anti-Israel policy with all this hostile attitude and attacks all the time. Maybe that's why Israel won't answer Deborah's letters. Listen! I'll turn the TV up a little. They're talking about Damascus."

"The state news agency said in Damascus today that the capital and much of southern Syria were plunged into darkness after a rebel attack struck a gas pipeline that supplies a power plant. Syrian rebels took control of Kindi Hospital near Aleppo after days of airstrikes on the opposition-held neighborhoods there in the north on Saturday. For more than a year the battle has raged between the government and the opposition for Aleppo. Kindi Hospital is close to the central prison on the edge of town where the government is holding thousands of detainees. The rebels holding the hospital are both the conservative Muslim groups and al-Qaida linked factions. Twenty-five rebels were killed in the battle over the hospital.

"Oh oh, I bet there's no power for electricity in Damascus now. I wonder how long it will take to fix it," wondered Vick. Hmmm, that means that computers won't be working. That's hard on the secret police.

They both heard honking from outside. "That must be Omar. I'm going out for a while, Nola. I'll be back later."

"At this hour? Be careful because of the curfew," she reminded him.

Vick got his jacket, nodded, kissed her good-bye and went out the door jogging the whole way to Omar's car. Nola turned on the porchlight and went to bed.

TWENTY-FOUR

Vick and Omar were on their way to see an illicit boxing match. Omar was planning on having Vick look it over and enter the ring to win the purse. He figured they could make an easy $5,000 which split in half, they surely both needed right now. He drove about twelve miles to the east and came to an empty warehouse. Vick followed Omar to a side door where Omar knocked three times. A little window opened at the top of the door and a face looked at them, asking in Arabic for their names which Omar gave. Then the door opened and a very black Nubian beckoned them in.

Following this man, they went down some dirty dark steps towards the smell of cigar smoke and the sound of men yelling. They came into a large room with a regular boxing arena was set up, ropes and all. The boxing match was just starting.

"God, Omar, whispered Vick." I haven't boxed for years. I'm out of shape. I don't know if I can still do it. I still weigh 95 kg. That's 209 pounds, you know. You can bill me as The Syrian Killer.

"You never lose your touch, Vick. You were a champion in Syria for a couple of years. You're still in good shape. Hell, you'll win for sure. Nobody can dodge those long arms of yours! You have a reach of 186 cm. You box with flair and passion."

"Just like I make love, Omar."

"Eight, nine, ten! He's out!" called the referee over a kid down on the floor. A veritable giant stood over him, the referee holding his arm up and calling him the winner. He was ready to take on the next boxer. That must have just been his warm up. The giant weighed at least 113.40 kg or 250 pounds and was a heavyweight like Muhammad Ali. He was at least 198.12 cm or 6'6". Vick was a heavy-weight too, but more on the Cruiser-weight side.

Vick had worn his tennis shoes on the trip, so all he had to do was step out of his trousers, which had a draw-string waistband, and pull off his shirt, and he jogged over to the ring and climbed in. The referee spoke to him for a few minutes, and the two men went to their corners. The bell rang and out they came, dancing around each other, feeling each other out. The giant let go with a left hook which Vick dodged, allowing him to let loose with his right which clipped the giant on his nose. He was huge, but not as lithe as Vick's 6'3", and Vick had a very long reach. The giant couldn't get close enough to hurt Vick. Being so tall, he was not as nimble. Vick let loose with another left hook and landed on the giant's jaw this time, causing him to go down for the count. The referee counted, "six, seven, eight, nine, and at ten the room exploded into a riot with policemen storming in the room who headed for the ring.

Vick had won the round and was expecting to be paid royally, but was whisked away by the police along with Omar and the referee and pushed up the stairs and into a police wagon and taken to the local jail. "Oh my God," moaned Vick. "This is some set-up"

After preliminary photos were taken of Vick and Omar, they were ushered into a cell with two others. Since it was already early morning, the two young men decided to just go to sleep and figure out what they had to do in the morning. Two cots were available so they laid down and fell asleep.

Morning came without any breakfast. Lunch time rolled around and they were finally ushered into an office and questioned. Since Vick had received no money, they couldn't hold him for practicing boxing professionally which was against the law in that building. The inquisitor was feeling very strange and was holding his head as he spoke to the two. He asked Vick if he knew the boxer from Syria by the name of Nasser al Shami. Vick told him he knew him and that he had won the bronze in 2004 in the Olympics in Athens that year, but that he had been shot in Homs by shot gun pellets in 2011 on July 4th by Assad's security forces along with 20 others. Vick mentioned to the policeman that he did not look well and asked him how he was feeling. The policeman looked at him in a surprised way, thought a minute, and told him, thinking that maybe he was a nurse or something like that. Actually, Vick was well versed in ailments, as back in Damascus, he grew herbs to cure all sorts of ailments. It was his family tradition. George knew what to take when you had a tummy ache or whatever ailed you. Besides that, he was trained in first aid as part of his safety engineering course.

Vick told the policeman to get some mint leaves and put in his tea with some honey, and take that three times every four hours and he would be feeling much better. The policeman smiled and thanked him. Then he decided to let the two go with a warning. They were not to repeat that performance. By doing this, he didn't have to fill out in triplicate a report about it, something that was so unimportant.

They walked out of the prison and the referee was also let go. He hailed a taxi for the three of them and they drove back to the warehouse where Vick and Omar were given their money. At last! They then got in Omar's rented car that was still in the parking lot and drove back home.

Word was out that if they waited for Egypt to pick them up for being over the time limit of staying in Egypt, they would be put in prison. So the two men decided to use their money for the short hop back to Lebanon and then get Vick's car and drive to Damascus. An hour later they arrived at Vick's apartment and Nola let them in. They immediately hit the sack and went back to sleep.

Nola was packed and ready to fly to her daughter's home and so Vick packed in the morning. He only had a few things anyway, his computer being one of them. He had his cell phone, something he had saved money to pay for this month but had no internet connection so hadn't been able to communicate with Deborah or his facebook friends. Rent, food, cell phone and that was it as far as his expenses went. He hadn't been communicating with Deborah except for the past two Wednesdays, and with his time limited, it was a very short note.

Deborah really missed hearing from him and had no idea what he was doing after knowing him so well for the past nine months. They had so much in common which was quite rare, considering their age differences. Both had fathers in the meat business. Vick was a boxer and so was Deborah's father. That connection sparked an interest in each other and made their relationship much closer. From then on, they found more and more things they shared. They each had skipped a year in school, for one thing. They were both interested in ancient Jewish history and shared the same opinions about Israel and politics. It was uncanny. Deborah wrote blogs defending Israel, and here was a partner, an Arabic speaker who agreed with her and could read what was going on in the Arab world. Now she just worried about how he was making it in the world after using up all the money he had after losing every single thing he ever had.

"Are we crazy or what considering going back into Syria?" asked Omar. I just heard a Doctors Without Borders report that over four days last week government airstrikes killed at least 189 people and wounded 879 others. God! Can we make it to your father's home alive and safe?"

"I don't know, Omar, but if we can, I can look for the gold that should be buried in the rubble and the gold plates. Maybe I can even find the box with papers in it about my mother."

"It'll be tricky sifting through all the mess without raising any suspicions." We'll have to do it at sunset or early evening and early morning when people aren't around."

"I don't think many people will be around anyway in the alley. There won't be any alley left, the way I hear it."

"Look, the gold was buried in the basement. Even if some of the debris has been cleared away, nobody would think to look under the ground or know about a basement. We might have to get a bulldozer or something, but I've got to go through with all this. It's going to make a difference in my destiny."

The next day Vick and Omar boarded a small plane and took off for Beirut. They landed and took a taxi to Vick's best friend's home while Vick texted him. Yes, he was home and his Mercedes was still safe and able to run. The three of them would drive to Damascus.

Going through the streets of Lebanon was a charge. They had to be so careful not to speed, and Vick was driving once again the car he loved so much and thought he'd never see again. Johnny had kept it safe from all comers by having a garage for it near his home. That was something most people didn't have. He had it locked and would go out periodically and start it up so the battery wouldn't run down. He was a mechanic as well, so anything that went wrong with it could be fixed. He didn't dare take it out on the streets or it would have been confiscated.

With three in the car, most would be coveters of the car didn't think about stopping them and highjacking the car, so they sailed into Damascus without any problem. Besides, all the ruckus going on was in Aleppo in northern Syria, not down in Damascus right now.

No electricity yet. The three ex-boy scouts were able to park the car in the deserted lane that used to be an alley where people would leave from their door and walk down in order to join a broader thoroughfare that led to a shopping area. Vick figured he had just parked outside of his father's home. No one came out to see who had driven up. Good.

They had a tent with them that Johnny had brought with him and set it up. Johnny had emptied his frig of food and the three had something to eat; cold lamb and milk and fresh fruit. Vick didn't drink any milk but ate heartily of the lamb. He'd hope the milk would be his breakfast if the others didn't finish it first. Whereas Vick would have drunk the milk, he remembered Deborah's teaching him that Jews didn't drink milk with a meat meal because that would have hurt the feelings of the mother cow or sheep since she had given her milk to people, and they would be eating her baby at the same time. How disgusting! That had cured him of ever doing that. In fact, even in the coffee house Vick had told the chef not to cook one of the recipes with milk since it contained meat and that's what the recipe had called for. He told him that it would cause bacteria and they didn't want people to come down with any stomach ailments after leaving the coffee house. He was making inroads into these Muslims, he had said.

Five days later, Vick, Omar and Johnny had cleared and had taken away tons of trash after finding a type of U Haul truck to cart away all the rubble that didn't amount to anything. So much of it seemed to be the roof of the home, and after that was lifted away, things got more interesting. Vick even found books in mint condition, so he knew he was in the vicinity of his father's study. "Vick, come here." I found it!" cried Omar. He held up a golden plate.

"Oh my God! It's, all right!" cried Vick. "I can't believe it! That thing is so solid and heavy!" They quickly opened the trunk of the Mercedes and put it in, covering it with a blanket that was still in there from Vick's using the blanket to lay down on the grass somewhere and make love to his present amour.

Only two hours later Vick was clearing away rubble with his gloved hand and felt something hard. He dug down with his fingers and felt a box. Could it be? He pulled it out of the rubble and it was a brown box engraved with dragons and flowers, it looked like. He brushed off the dust and tried to open it up as the other two crowded around him to see what was inside. It opened after a little tugging. There on top was the picture of his mother! Vick started to tremble as he took off his gloves and picked it up and looked at his mother for the first time in his life. She was indeed a beautiful lady.

"Wow! What a beaut!" exclaimed Omar. "No wonder your dad went after her." Okay, Vick, let's see what else is in there. Vick put the picture down carefully and searched through the rest of the papers which held her vital statistics. She was Liliane Cohen and was born in 1955. That meant she was twenty-five years old when Vick was born. To Vick, it meant that there hadn't been any suitor in her life from the Jewish community and was not surprised that she relented and fell for his Muslim father. A Cohen! That also meant that he could have the J1c3d haplogroup! He didn't realize the Cohen gene had to be from his father. Oh, this was worth coming back to Damascus for. To him it meant more than getting his Mercedes back in mint condition. Oh my God!

The trio were quite tired from all the digging and had decided after eating more cold food including lots of pita and humous to flag it now and sleep with one on watch. They had a gun with them. Omar took the first watch, and then Vick, and finally Johnny would be awake.

Morning came and they all were ready to discover the basement. From where the study was that they had been digging through, Vick figured out where the stairs to the basement would have been, and they moved to another corner of the rubble and started digging there. About four hours later they made progress which was in removing the roof remains and getting down past the dust and pieces of wood and plaster to hit paydirt; the steps leading down to the basement. It was like finding the entrance to King Tut's tomb! They opened the basement door and walked in carrying a flashlight.

"Here is the spot where I had dug before. I know that under this dirt is a pile of gold."

"Wish we had a shovel."

"Omar, look! There's the shovel I had used still sitting in the corner."

Johnny grabbed the shovel and started digging. It wasn't long till he gave it to Omar who continued and finally handed it to Vick. He only had to dig about five more minutes and they saw gold shining in the flashlight's rays. It was real and was there! It wasn't a dream of Vick's after all. He was more surprised than they were. The geni had led him here in the first place!

The three-some started hauling up gold bars up the steps and out to the trunk of the car. One stood there guarding the car while the other two walked back to retrieve more bars, and then they traded positions, which gave one person a break from all the walking and climbing and carrying the heavy bars. Finally the trunk was full and the lode was empty. They had done it!

They were rich! Vick had promised his two friends each 25% which left him with 50% of the total value of the treasure.

TWENTY-FIVE

What do you do with gold bars and gold plates in the middle of a war zone which is littered with debris that hadn't been cleared and where electricity is non-existent? How do you turn them into cash! That's where Vick's talents came in. He had contacts in Damascus from his smuggling days. He could handle life here. He dialed a number on his cell phone from memory, the only one he had stored in his mind since it was a regular one, and made contact.

"Salaam, Anas. How are you? Good. I have produce to sell. Are you ready to buy?"

Twelve hours later the trio sat in a coffee shop that was still intact in Damascus and ordered a big meal that included lots of lamb for the hungry men. Vick felt that his jabs were much longer and stronger when he had eaten plenty of meat, and he thought that his plan might be including fighting before it reached fruition.

They were well sated with food and cash in their wallets, ready to embark on Vick's last part of the plan. He now knew his mother's last name and had reason to believe that he could enter Israel, so they left the shop and started on a route. Vick was going to try to enter Israel through the Golan Heights that was populated by 20,000 Druze of which Vick's father might have been descended from with a 25% chance being there were Halabi's that were Druze. Many Druze continued to be loyal to Assad. The village of Quneitra in the Golan was only thirty-one miles from Damascus, so that's where they would drive and leave Vick. Johnny would take the car and he and Omar would drive back to Beirut with it.

Vick had heard of stories about Syrians that were injured crossing over into Israel and they had been taken to hospitals there. He thought if worse came to worse, he might have an accident and be found and taken into Israel. One story he heard was about a pregnant lady who was taken in and her baby was born in Israel making the baby an Israeli citizen and of course she would be able to stay, too. "Lucky lady," he thought. Another story was about a fifteen year old boy who arrived at the hospital in Safed with a missing hand and both eyes injured. Both eyeballs were totally shattered. Their trauma center for the past ten months has been receiving casualties from Syria. They've been men, women and children and some so badly hurt that doctors there have never seen the likes of such horrific injuries, and they're veterans used to administering to war casualties because these injuries are on civilians and not soldiers dressed for combat with helmets and such to protect them.

Forty minutes later they arrived in Quneitra only to see that the Free Syrian Army was up and about in this place. The Golan itself was a rocky plateau high up which was why Israel needed to hold on to it for security reasons. It's where the Syrians had bombarded Israeli towns below, being it's about 3,300 feet high or 1,000 meters. Mt. Hermon, a favorite skiing area is in the Golan. That's enough reason to want to have it as part of Israel, as many Israelis love to ski. About three million tourists per year come to the Golan as it includes a Game Reserve center in Gamla. The area has a canyon, waterfalls and trails. One can even run into raptors, even rare ones.

After checking their map, they saw that Quneitra was only twelve and a half miles or twenty kilometers from Meron, which was a famous town where they celebrated the holiday of Lag B'Omer. That would be Vick's destination to make contact with Israelis and declare the right of return.

They could also run into Israelis, so this is where Vick left his friends, wished them a safe trip and started walking with a back pack that Johnny had brought along on his back. So far so good. He looked like any other Druse. It would be an arduous hike of almost thirteen miles, but Vick was in good condition, though he was a little winded from years of smoking. Funny, he didn't miss smoking right now out in this 40 degree F or 4.44 C weather. It was crisp and so to his liking. Gosh, he'd love to live here.

Five hours later, Vick made it to Meron without being stopped, though he had to take a few rest stops. Looking out for other hikers, he managed to spot an eagle high up, probably over Gamla, the Game Reserve. He'd love to come back and hike through that spot. What a wonderful world this was! It was lovely and had the perfect temperature! How he'd love to share this with Deborah!

Suddenly a trio of three IDF soldiers called out to him to stop in Hebrew. Hafseek! That was a word he had not learned from Deborah as yet, but he recognized it as not being Arabic, and stopped. The men walked over to him and asked to see his ID. Having no Israeli papers, he pulled out his passport and saw their jaws drop and their stance changed. "Anee Yehudi," Vick explained in his only Hebrew. "Anee Yehudi. Eema sheli Yehudi, Liliane Cohen. Bevakasha, I want to make aliyah and am asking for the law of return!" he pleaded. "Yehudi, yehudi!" He pulled out his box and showed the three soldiers its contents. "Eema, eema shelee," he boasted.

All three smiled and shook hands with him and motioned that he was to follow them. They drove to their station and explained their new mission to their captain and continued driving Vick to Zfat, which Deborah had told him about because she had lived there for five years. From Zfat, another driver took over and put Vick in a van and continued driving to Jerusalem where he was ushered into the police station and put in a waiting cell. Dinner was served to him by a private through a section of the door that slid open.

Finally a captain walked in and asked if Vick could speak anything other than Hebrew. Vick got the idea and answered in Arabic and then in English. The captain could speak both easily and started questioning him in Arabic. He wrote out his report and then ushered Vick into another cell with a cot.

After a week, Vick was wondering what he did wrong. He still had his wallet and money, thank God, which was pretty amazing. If he were in any other prison in Syria, Lebanon or Egypt, he imagined he would have lost it all. They had checked him and had taken away his gun.

Finally, he was brought before a commission who spoke with him and welcomed him as a new Israeli Jew, an ole khadash. They brought out some wine and made a toast, "L'Chaim! To life!"

Yes, to life! Vick knew what he had to do now. Get back on line and tell Deborah all about it and see if she could join him now. He had told her that he wanted her to live with him in Israel because her family didn't appreciate her. At least she could come stay with him for a month to help him get oriented. To do that he had to get back online and had all the money in the world to do that. He wanted to contact Rabbi Hamra and convert even though it wasn't necessary now that he knew who his mother was, a Cohen. He wanted to know about Judaism as much as possible, and, the big thing, he wanted to join the army, the IDF. To top it off, he had noticed a beautiful red-headed sergeant in the other room, and thought maybe she might help him out before he left this building. Surely they weren't going to just turn him loose, were they?

"Shalom," he said with a smile to the red-headed sergeant. "Do you speak English?" he asked her.

"Of course," she replied. I'm an American-Israeli. "How are you?"

"So happy," he replied. So very happy!"

The captain of the IDF office smiled and thought of the memo they kept on the bulletin board about this Amram that an American-Israeli had alerted them about being Jewish and wanting to move to Israel. He had received thirty such notices from various offices about him. They thought that if he ever made it this far without being killed, he would be truly remarkable. Rabbi Hamra was eager to meet him. That was the surprise they had in store for him after he visited with Tali Halal outside at her desk. From there they will take him to a Merkaz ha Klitta where he will live for three months and learn Hebrew and go on a few field trips to see Israel. It is to be the one in Haifa.

"He'll love that, being it's on the sea. We'll get him in the navy, I think," thought Captain. Naman. "I've read the letters his friend sent to us all about him. He's a diver. Goes down 150 feet."

"Amram was the father of Moses. This guy might father some great person as well. You never know." Amram spoke about wanting a DNA test right away. I'll be interested to see what genes he does carry from his father, and we know his mother was a Cohen, so she had lots of Cohen genes to pass onto him as well. At least one-fourth of his genes are Cohen. That reminds me, I'll nudge him to order a kit right away."

"Amram, remember, you wanted to order......"

"I already did it, Captain. Thank you. Tali has already told me about the Mercaz and gave me the addreses. I ordered the kit and it will be delivered there. This is the same Mercaz that my friend, Deborah stayed in for ten months. I'm ready to start my new life!"

Major Biton walked in the office and spoke with the Captain while Vick was still there. He overheard them speak in Hebrew but couldn't make out what they were saying. The Major's voice raised and he seemed rather angry, then walked out.

Captain Naman spoke to Vick and told him that problems had arisen in the Sudan where the Muslim Brotherhood was trying to take over through Malik and Hussein Obama, relatives of President Obama of the USA. They had had refugees enter Israel from the Sudan recently and it was a big problem. What's going on is that they are recruiting young men with something like $5,000 American dollars to join their people. It's causing problems in Egypt who have their own problems right now. Everything in crazy

"What's happening in Egypt right now?" asked Vick. I've been living there for the past two years."

"Big matters." It's just been found out that Morsi gave away security secrets of Egypt to Iran. This is high treason. Now Egypt been hit with suicide bombers all over the place, with some one hundred fifty being injured and in hospital, and others killed. Bombers were in Cairo on a bus. Oy! Everything is happening at once. Vick, you don't have much time. Report to the Ulpan and then," He stopped short as he wrote out a note and handed it to Vick. "Give this to the housemother and have somebody take you to the Navy. Sign up quickly. We may need your talents in diving or whatever. Be sure you get checked out by the doctor there. See you later!"

"Yes, sir!" Vick walked out and found Tali. She grabbed her jacket and they walked out of the building towards her vehicle.

References

http://www.hrw.org/news/2013/11/10/egypt-syria-refugees-detained-coerced-return

Resource: http://en.wikipedia.org/wiki/Syrian_Civil_War

http://www.newrepublic.com/article/115017/syrian-refugees-egypt-unluckiest-people-earth

http://altreligion.about.com/od/symbols/ig/Pentagrams/Samael-Lilith-Pentagram.htm

http://www.jewishgen.org/sefardsig/aleppojews.htm

http://www.reuters.com/article/2013/12/11/us-syria-crisis-usa-idUSBRE9BA08820131211

http://freebeacon.com/videos-show-egyptian-president-inciting-hatred-of-jews-israel/http://www.haaretz.com/news/middle-east/1.541989

http://www.nytimes.com/2011/02/12/world/middleeast/12egypt.html?pagewanted=all&_r=0

http://www.mercycorps.org/articles/iraq-jordan-lebanon-syria/quick-facts-what-you-need-know-about-syrian-refugee-crisis

http://en.wikipedia.org/wiki/List_of_massacres_in_Syria

http://en.wikipedia.org/wiki/Hama

http://en.wikipedia.org/wiki/Hafez_al-Assad

http://www.armscontrol.org/factsheets/Timeline-of-Syrian-Chemical-Weapons-Activity

http://en.metapedia.org/wiki/Jewish_ritual_murder

http://www.ncbi.nlm.nih.gov/pmc/articles/PMC1530136/

http://america.aljazeera.com/watch/shows/america-tonight/america-tonight-blog/2013/10/8/why-isn-t-americatakinginmoresyrianrefugees.html

http://www.haaretz.com/misc/article-print-page/golan-heights-druze-start-to-turn-against-syria-s-assad-1.454167?trailingPath=2.169%2C2.216%2C2.217%2C

Myths and Facts-a concise record of the Arab-Israeli conflict by Dr. Mitchell G. Bard, Joel Himelfarb

http://www.kurdmedia.com/article.aspx?id=13837

http://en.wikipedia.org/wiki/Taba,_Egypt

http://www.youtube.com/watch?v=iEseJViidy8

http://www.jewishjournal.com/world/article/the_forgotten_refugees_of_ghouta_syria

Oregonian newspaper 12/15/13, page A13 ships to haul out chemicals

http://en.wikipedia.org/wiki/Economy_of_Syria

http://en.wikipedia.org/wiki/List_of_countries_by_oil_production

http://www.economist.com/blogs/economist-explains/2013/12/economist-explains-0

The Strong Horse, Power, politics, and the Clash of Arab Civilizations by Lee Smith

http://middleeast.about.com/od/syria/f/hama-rules.htm

http://www.haaretz.com/misc/article-print-page/.premium-1.554424?trailingPath=2.169%2C2.212%2C2.215%2C

http://jewishbubba.blogspot.com/2013/10/why-protocols-of-elders-of-zion-is-anti.html

http://www.reuters.com/article/2013/09/12/us-syria-crisis-egypt-refugees-idUSBRE98B0OE20130912

http://en.wikipedia.org/wiki/Refugees_of_the_Syrian_Civil_War

http://www.discoverthenetworks.org/printgroupProfile.asp?grpid=6204

http://middleeast.about.com/od/syria/f/hama-rules.htm

http://www.dailypaul.com/297409/what-has-bashar-al-assad-done

http://www.telegraph.co.uk/news/worldnews/europe/sweden/7278532/Jews-leave-Swedish-city-after-sharp-rise-in-anti-Semitic-hate-crimes.htmlhttp://www.telegraph.co.uk/news/worldnews/europe/sweden/7278532/Jews-leave-Swedish-city-after-sharp-rise-in-anti-Semitic-hate-crimes.html

http://faculty-staff.ou.edu/L/Joshua.M.Landis-1/syriablog/2005/10/jews-of-syria-by-robert-tuttle.htm

Epilogue

This book never would have come about had it not been for Vick's desire to be remembered and share his life with me. I told him that he had to write his story, and though he is quite a fluent English speaker, would have found it difficult to write a book in English. The ending is the only thing not true. He is still facing the fear of being deported to a refugee camp as Egypt is busy rounding Syrians up. However, the latest news is that as the first of February, he will be sent back to Syria. He was refused a residency status for Egypt.

After working hard to earn money to go to Sweden, as his stay in Egypt was up and not wanting to go to a refugee camp, Vick worked so hard that when he arrived home, he collapsed with a stroke. His friend, Wilson, the doctor, arrived at his home after being telephoned and took him to the hospital. This young man must have an operation that he can't afford to remove a blood clot. His leg is paralzyed now. He has been told that he can no longer dive. The free health insurance promised by Morsi no longer exists as it stopped with Morsi's removal from office. My ending is Vic's wish to live and marry in Israel.